A Sight Unseen

Written By

Craig R Key

Edited By

Maggie Douglas   Jerry Hart   Courtney Smith

ISBN: 9780578147383

This book is dedicated to my supportive family, friends, editors, but most of all to my father who lost his battle with pancreatic cancer on May 1st 2014. An inspiring, compassionate man. He's with God, whom I also owe my thanks.

Prologue

Many human and elven soldiers were unaware of what had started the war between them. All they knew was that they were to not let the other side win. The elves had nature, and magic on their side, while the humans had more men and stronger weapons. This made them rather evenly matched, but both sides had lost so many.

Separ was a young human soldier in the army of The Kingdom Alliance. At the time, Separ was a slender boy on the cusp of adulthood, and was completely new to the concept of killing as a means to make coin. He was fresh faced, and his brown hair rested on his shoulders.

It was hardly his choice to be a soldier seeing as how he lived in the deserts of the Southern Continents, and they were always scrounging for food and water. He would either die in the desert, or live healthy as a soldier. Plus, he knew that elves wanted to avoid the Southern Continents due to lack of vegetation, so he was sure he would never see a battle. However, this theory of his was proven wrong.

Two moon cycles after Separ had joined the fight, a battle found its way to Fort Glory where he was stationed. The elves knew most of the Kingdom Alliance's weapons were created in the desert, where some of the finest smiths studied. To cut off the human army's supplies, this is where the elves would have to strike.

Before the sun could rise, elven archers took down the men in the watch towers, warriors scaled the walls, and mages tunneled under the wall using their spells to control the earth around them. This all happened before any of the humans were aware that they were under attack.

A lone soldier noticed the siege just as he was returning from the latrines, and he managed to run back to the bunks unnoticed.

Most of the other soldiers had drifted off to sleep, but Separ was still conscious as the lone soldier ran into the room crying, "We are under attack!"

Separ instantly pulled his sword from his sheath laying at his bedside. He had no desire to kill elves or anyone, but he was certainly no coward when it came to fighting for his life.

"Where is the attack coming from?" asked Separ.

"Everywhere. It's coming from—"

Suddenly, the lone soldier was silenced by an arrow to his back. He collapsed, revealing an elf in full armor with a long-bow in his hand. The armor was a mixture of wood, leather, and metal formed tight to the body, and seemed to not be shaped by hands. As if pulled naturally from the earth, it curved around the elves allowing natural, quick movements like pulling an arrow from the quiver in less time than it would take a human to even pull a sword.

The archer swiftly pulled another arrow back on the bow, but Separ rolled under his cot just as the arrow impaled the bedding. The head of the projectile stopped inches from the young soldier's face, and he instantly lifted the cot to block another arrow while he got to his feet. He threw his bed at the elf, deflecting another projectile as he ran within striking distance. Separ swung his sword, cutting the bow in two, and the archer pulled a dagger. The young human parried the dagger, and buried his blade into the elf where his neck met his shoulder.

The archer fell lifeless just as the five remaining human soldiers were coming into a confused consciousness, so Separ pulled his sword free, and turned to the men uttering, "Don't just lay there. To arms!"

After just moments, the humans were dressed and armed for combat. They ran from the bunk to see the bodies of their allies dead, and the rest of them putting up a futile fight against the outnumbering elves. Separ raised his weapon over his head, let out a battle cry, and ran to the aid of his brothers, followed by the soldiers from his bunk.

The elven warriors fell, but not before taking the lives of most of the humans at Fort Glory. Separ was the only man alive with a higher rank than the other ten survivors as the sun began to rise. He had never seen himself as a leader, nor did he want it. But now he had no choice. His soldiers looked to him for orders, and he was not going to disappoint.

Separ decided that the battle had not ended when he found one of the mages' tunnels with the footsteps of retreating elves leading into it. As the sun lit up the faces of the fallen men, Separ decided these elves had to pay for the death of so many humans this day.

"The wounded will stay here! You've fought well!" shouted Separ. "As for the rest of you, we are hunting down the cowards!"

The men cheered as they followed their new leader into the tunnel with a bloodlust that they had never felt before. They marched in the dark for what seemed like an eternity, but as they saw the morning light peering through the other side, their footsteps picked up speed. The men had a hunger for death, and Separ was sure to prepare a feast fit to satisfy even the largest horde of giants.

The men peered out from the tunnel which opened at the side of a mountain, and they could see a small elven camp nearby. Wounded warriors crouched at the feet of a mage, who had his staff raised over his head. Blue wisps of light slithered out of the orb atop his staff, and found their way to the open gashes in the elves' flesh as the mage chanted in his language.

Separ turned to his men whispering, "We attack now, before they can mend their wounds. Leave the mage to me."

With that the humans burst from the cave screaming waves of panic into the elves. The melee began as Separ charged the mage, who attempted to slow the mighty soldier with flame cast from his hand.

Separ leapt out of the way of the projectile, and noticed that he was next to a small pot of a sticky flammable liquid that was used in making flaming arrows. Instantly, the young soldier grabbed the pot, got to his feet and hurled it at the mage. Just as the elf summoned another flame, the liquid ignited in front of him. The fire wrapped around the mage, embracing him into death. He screamed and writhed until he finally lost consciousness, becoming a pile of smoldering flesh.

As Separ looked to the rest of his men, he saw that they were victorious. The humans raised their weapons high, and shouted the remainder of their adrenaline out of their bodies.

They searched the camp for any information that could be used to crush more of the elven forces, but what they found only set in motion Separ's thirst for power. A written instruction to tame a creature for use of war, and a map showing the location of an island near the Northern Continent inhabited by only dragons.

Having proved himself a mighty warrior, The Kingdom Alliance granted Separ and his men to go to the island of dragons. Controlling dragons would prove a great asset to the humans in the war against the elves, so not long after the victory at Fort Glory, they set sail to the island.

It was only one moon cycle before the human ships met the shores of the island, and with the help of the elven map, the men had no trouble finding the caves leading to the nests of the dragons.

The trek through the snow and ice did not freeze the strong spirits of Separ's men. However, they became reluctant after seeing the burnt bodies of several elves lining the floor of the tunnel further than the sunlight would show. As they advanced deeper in the ground, the torches revealed even more corpses. If any elven life was spared, it was clear they would be few, and they would be no threat to the human soldiers.

Only losing their way once in the winding tunnels, they eventually reached the glowing entrance to the center of the island deep inside the mountain. The smell of sour decay and sulfur became stronger with every step. The men began shedding their armor and furs due to the practically unbearable rising temperatures. Once they entered the doorway, they could see the reason for the heat.

Thin, natural stone bridges stretched from every opening in the walls over boiling lava, which lit the room a bright red. The stone walkways waved in the extreme heat, and connected in the center platform where an elven mage was forcefully pulling a young elven woman to an altar. Even over the rumbling of the lava below her screeching pleas could be heard.

"Halt!" cried Separ as he approached the center platform on one of the thin stone bridges. "And I suggest you let her go."

Without a word, the mage tossed her to the ground, but as he slammed the bottom of his staff on the ground, it was clear surrender wasn't his intention. Three of the bridges began to quake, including the one the soldiers were on.

Three of the humans stumbled off the loosening stone falling to their doom in the lava below, their skin charring and splitting before splashing into the bright molten rock. Two of the remaining soldiers and Separ dove to the platform as the bridge collapsed under them and the rest of his men retreated into the entrance with nowhere to go.

One of the soldiers landed on the platform, the other hit the ledge, and his grip was slipping. Separ grabbed hold of the rocks below the platform, and after dropping his sword, he pushed his soldier on the ledge, which allowed the human to get to his feet.

As Separ climbed to safety, the mage struck one of the men with his staff, knocking him off the platform to his demise. The remaining soldier slashed the staff in two, which caused a pulse that knocked both the mage and soldier to the ground.

Separ climbed atop the platform before the mage could get upright, and he lifted the elf by the hood on his robe.

He threw the mage onto the altar with a blood thirsty scream, and began to repeatedly slam his fist into the skull of the elf. He only stopped beating the mage when he saw his soldier raise his sword to the young elven woman.

"No!" Separ ordered.

"But she's one of them, sir!" said the human as he lowered his blade.

"They are our enemies. And hers."

Before they could argue over her life any further, the lava cavern became loud with sounds of screeching creatures. In the distance, through the waves of heat, the horned and scaly heads of several dragons peered out of the caves. Their eyes turned toward the center platform, and their thin lips curled away from their pointed teeth.

Separ knew there was only one way out of this alive, so he turned to the bloody and broken mage, and growled, "How do we control the dragons!?!"

"You need the Eye of Sight Unseen," sputtered the beaten elf through his crimson coated lips, "and you will never have it. We will die together."

The mage choked out a laugh, while the dragons wrapped their large, boney claws around the edges of the stone bridges, slowly inching toward the center platform. As for the men waiting helpless at one of the entryways, they met their end from an unexpected flame rising behind them from the belly of one of the stealthy, scale-covered, and winged beasts.

"The altar!" uttered the young elf woman. "It requires a sacrifice."

Separ turned to her, then back to the mage, whose eyes widened as the mighty soldier picked up one of the pieces of the broken staff from the ground.

"No!" was the last word the bloody elf could say before Separ drove the broken wood through his chest.

The body went limp, as the mage's life poured upon the altar. The dragons still advanced closer, but no one could look away from the bright light peeking from around the edge of the staff in the corpse's wound. Suddenly, the broken wood flew out of the chest of the mage, and fell into the lava below. A beam of radiant light flashed out of the bleeding hole, and slowly a small, red, crystal orb emerged from the light hovering just above the body.

The remaining soldier and the elf woman turned to the dragons, who had finally reached the platform and had begun circling for an attack. He brought up his sword ready to futilely defend himself as she moved behind him. The dragons raised their heads, and took a deep breath, preparing to exhale flame.

Separ reached out and wrapped his hands around the Eye of Sight Unseen, and instantly the dragons ceased their attack. He slowly turned to the dragons, and couldn't believe all the reptilian pupils that were locked on him, as if waiting for his command. Never had Separ felt as powerful as he did that day. Never had he felt so in control.

With a smile slowly crossing his face, he raised the orb in the air, and the dragons bowed to their new leader; Separ: The Dragon Voice.

Chapter I

aim awoke. He did this, as he did every morning, with the rooster's call. Most could ignore this sound, and wait for the castle bells, but Saim found this difficult as he slept in a small shanty near the chicken coop. His eyes adjusted to the bluish light spilling through the spaces in the warped wooden boards acting as his walls, and he brushed the loose hay from his moist brow. It was going to be a hot day seeing as the sun had just barely peeked over the land, and already Saim felt as if his body was mimicking a steamy bog.

His back sore from the farm work the day before, he managed to sit up with a groan. Glancing at the hay pile that served as his bed, he saw that the straw was strewn in every direction on the dirt floor, confirming his suspicions that he had another restless night of sleep. Wiping the grit from his eyes, the vivid memory of his nightmare came flooding back to mind as he shuddered.

Night after night, Saim dreamed of his mother. He had known her less than a third of his life, but her kind elven eyes and soft, soothing voice stayed with him. Saim remembered her, but with his age of about twenty-one years, he was finding it increasingly harder to remember the details of her appearance. He wasn't even sure of his age, since the last birthday he celebrated was with her.

...

In the dream, he is scared, and so is his mother, Lurya. She wears a brave face as she runs through the woods with him clutched tightly in her arms. Saim is just a child, but he dares not cry aloud. His mother pleads with him not to do so, and he won't let her down. He is her brave boy.

"My brave baby boy," she whispers to him over and over again.

And that is the last night he will ever see her.

...

Saim ran his fingers through his dirty, long, brown hair to shake loose the hay clinging to the oily strands. His fingertips grazed the jagged scars atop his ears, forcing an unpleasant, faded memory of his caretaker when he was without his mother. His appointed guardian was a womanizing traveling bard. A human by the name of Havish.

...

One night, not long after he took in the child, Havish pulled a dagger he had in his belt, placed it in the fire he had built for the campsite, and poured water from his canteen over the hot blade, causing it to sizzle.

"I know you cannot imagine it now, but this is for your own good, boy," he grumbled under his mead-tainted breath. Saim couldn't recall a moment that Havish hadn't had the smell of the fools' drink on his being, but this night it was particularly pungent.

Tears rolled down Saim's youthful, chubby cheeks as Havish approached with the steaming dagger.

"Close your eyes, child." Havish's voice shook, as did the blade in his hands. "It will only hurt for a moment."

Saim shut his eyes as tightly as he could, but he opened them when Havish grabbed the tip of his pointed ear.

"No," Saim cried.

"I'm so sorry," Havish whispered. Then with a quick swipe of the dagger, the pointed tip of Saim's ear was gone.

A scream boiled up from the back of Saim's small throat, but before the shout reached the pinnacle of its volume, Havish placed his hand over the half-elf's mouth. Saim's jaw still hung open in a scream, but shut after the taste of his own blood tickled the tip of his tongue.

"One down," Havish slurred, "one to go."

...

Saim exited his shanty while adjusting his shirt and looked out over the vegetable fields just past the chicken coop. He took his first breath of the warm outside air, turning his gaze to the kingdom of Cresience, silhouetted by the sun rising behind it. An ordinary man would be moved by such beauty, but to a half-elf who had never known a home of his own, he could take it or leave it.

The vegetables were ripe for harvesting, so Saim thought he would get a lead on his workload while his employer, an elderly human by the name of Gormah, slept.

Potatoes would be the first crop since they required the most bending to retrieve. This would give Saim's aching back a chance to relax as the rest of the day went on.

He leaned back into his shanty to pick up a sack, and some rope to affix it to his back. This wasn't the orthodox way to collect potatoes, but he could carry twice the amount before having to break to empty his pouch. He was a crafty lad, but one would never know if they listened to the things that people would whisper when he walked within the walls of Cresience.

At the end of every harvest, Saim accompanied his employer to sell them in the nearby kingdom. Saim knew that elves, let alone half-elves, were not to enter the kingdom, nor any human settlement or village. Elves were to stay in the forests away from human taint, but half-elves were considered abominations to both the elves and humans alike. Mixing breeds was seen as great of a sin as laying with beasts to almost all races across the land. For that reason, Saim knew that he had no place in the world. However, his trimmed ears, lanky hair, and hooded cloak made it easier to blend in.

He tried hard to remain above the gaze of suspicion, but this caused him to keep his head down and stay quiet. Naturally, this did in fact conjure mild suspicion, but mostly led others to believe he was simple, causing mockery of his intelligence. Common belief seemed to be that having no desire to speak made him a dullard, though Saim found that those who spoke the most had less intelligent things to say.

With a sigh, Saim tied a knot in the rope around his chest. It was a knot he remembered from childhood, but he couldn't remember where or when he learned it. He just managed to absorb it into his youthful, untainted mind. Before fear. Before pain. Before loneliness. Before hopelessness.

He closed his eyes and shook his head as if to ward off any sad thoughts, inhaled deeply while opening his eyes, and walked to the potato fields.

The day grew hotter and hotter as he worked, and when the sun cast a smaller shadow at his feet, Saim knew it had to be at least noon. He dropped the last potato in the large sack on his back, and wiped the sweat off his brow with his forearm. There had yet to be any sign of Gormah.

The half-elf found Gormah to be a kindly old man, but Saim also wasn't aware that the man paid much less than other farmers in the land. If Saim knew, he would assume this was all the old man could afford to pay a farm hand, but Gormah actually paid so little to ensure that Saim would not be able to afford trekking anywhere else. Saim was the hardest worker that he had ever seen, and he wasn't about to lose that commodity to another farmer.

Saim toyed with the thought of not waking Gormah, and just finishing out the day himself. However, this would probably result in a tongue-lashing, so he decided he might just do it without the old man.

After walking up the trail to the farmhouse, the half-elf instantly noticed how quiet things seemed. Of course, there were the sounds of the chickens and the gentle song of the birds in the distance, but it was the lack of noise between those moments that seemed eerie.

Saim shrugged off the uneasy feeling along with the sack on his back, setting it on the wooden porch. After rolling the tensions of the already-hard workday out of his neck and shoulders, he softly rapped on the door.

No answer.

Saim knocked once more, and shouted, "Gormah?"

Again, no answer.

Saim, lowered his head, and sighed. Waking Gormah from slumber was enough to get shouted at for hours.

Saim opened the door slowly so as to not wake Gormah too suddenly. He was going to try a much gentler approach to this. The hinges of the door were not doing stealth any favors as it creaked with every inch.

Finally, the door was open just enough for Saim's slender frame to slip through. He sucked in what little stomach he had, and squeezed through the small gap, only letting out a small breath of relief.

He took a moment to enjoy his small victory and inhaled as deep as he could. Saim slowly began to tip-toe to Gormah's bedroom while holding his breath to listen closely to the sounds of his movements. Every squeak of the floorboards might as well have been a shriek of terror in Saim's misshapen ears. Truth be told, he excelled at stealthiness, and it had saved his life more than once.

...

Later in the night, after Havish had permanently deformed young Saim's ears and proceeded to drink himself into a deep sleep, Saim opened his eyes. He pretended to be resting soundly, but the pain throbbing through the bloody bandages on the sides of his head made sleep an impossibility.

The child lie still in the dirt next to Havish and glared at him until he was sure the bard was asleep. As soon as the snores began to cut through the quiet night air, and almost drowned out the crackling of the campfire, Saim sat up.

This human, a poor excuse for a bard, had caused great pain to a child that had recently been abandoned by his own mother. Saim, even at this young age knew that enough was enough. He was leaving, and he was finding his mother.

He got to his feet slowly and quietly, and moved over to bard's wagon. All was quiet, except for a soft snort of Havish's horse, which almost caused the child to jump out of his shoes. Saim quickly covered his mouth to muffle his startled gasp, and continued to the wagon.

He carefully grabbed a small bag of salted swine meats and the extra canteen from the wagon. He knew even at this age he had to travel light, so he couldn't carry much more.

He climbed out of the back of the wagon and turned to leave the side of this bard once and for all. However, the dim light managed to reflect off of something metal on Havish's belt. The dagger used on Saim's small ears had almost fallen out of its sheath.

The young half-elf took a deep breath and crept to Havish. Saim knelt beside him, watching his chest lift and fall. With the rhythm of the snores memorized, the child gripped the handle of the blade. With every loud breath, Saim pulled the blade out bit by bit.

Suddenly, Havish shifted from his back to his side, freeing the dagger from the sheath and placing it into young Saim's possession. He looked at the blade almost in disbelief that he wasn't caught taking it, noticing the dried blood on the tip.

He could have left at that very moment, but for what felt like hours, Saim stood over the bard's resting body. This bastard hurt him, and he knew that he would always remember this every time he saw or felt his ears. The child's grip tightened around the handle. It wasn't the decision to end this man's life, but rather where to thrust the blade, that seemed daunting.

With a sigh, Saim realized he didn't have it in his heart, no matter how justified it may be. He tucked the dagger in his belt and left. He was a free half-elf, and no one would ever hurt him again.

...

Saim inched closer and closer to Gormah's door, and he was finally close enough to reach the handle. That's when he noticed the door hung slightly ajar. Another deep breath, and Saim was prepared to open the door.

With two fingers, he slowly guided the door open, but stopped immediately as he heard a bottle hit the floorboards. He cursed himself with a whisper and stepped into the room, reaching down for the rolling bottle of wine that was leaving a trail of liquid from the door to the middle of Gormah's bedroom.

After picking the bottle up, he looked at the spilled wine and grimaced, realizing this was just another reason for the old man to complain. However, after a quick glance to Gormah's motionless body near the bed, Saim wondered if the scolding would ever come.

"Gormah?" Saim's voice cracked.

After a few moments, he realized Gormah had not taken a breath. He knelt down beside his employer and nudged him.

No sound. No movement.

Saim reached for Gormah's hand, but jerked back with a gasp as his fingers grazed the skin. The old man was cold. Freezing. Lifeless.

After rolling Gormah over, Saim glared at his swollen purple face, eyes like milky gems, and dried remnants of the coughed-up meal he had eaten the night before on his gray beard, shirt, and floor.

Saim collapsed backward against the wall, staring in disbelief at the corpse. Where remorse should have manifested, Saim could only feel worry: worry over how he would live without work, and worry over the idea that somehow he would be blamed.

His instincts, though he often ignored them, were rarely wrong.

Chapter II

With an unfortunate message to deliver, Saim followed the trail to the gates of Cresience. Its tall castle towers peeked over the stone walls, and grew closer as the half-elf closed distance to the archway, which was guarded by two members of the Cresience army.

Gormah's horse, which Gormah had never bothered to name, pulled back on the reins with every step Saim took. He didn't dare ride his master's horse, but Saim felt it necessary to at least lead her to the kingdom in case Gormah's son, Micah, needed a quick way to reach the farm.

Micah worked at a tavern called The Pewter Flagon not far from the entrance. Saim only met him in person once, a few months before. He was a boorish and bigoted man whose appearance matched his personality. Most of the things he had to say involved how successful he was, bragging of good pay and more drunken wenches than he knew what to do with. This all seemed a bit unbelievable to Saim. With a practically toothless grin and a patchy orange beard, Micah didn't really seem like he was as sought after by women. His personality was even less desirable. It seemed he could not get through five sentences without referring to elves in a negative light. They were to blame for slow business at the tavern, supplies coming in late, the spread of disease, and somehow even the bad weather.

"Easy," Saim grumbled at the struggling horse. "You'll be going back home soon enough."

This didn't seem to comfort the her, but she trusted Saim due to all the time they had spent together in the fields, and it was always him that brought her food and water. Saim somehow felt her uneasiness, agreeing with her reluctance to enter the walls of Cresience. All he could do was solemnly hope for the trip to be smooth and over quickly, without ridicule.

As soon as Saim reached the gate, one of the guards turned toward him and greeted, "Hello, traveler."

Saim looked out from under his hood, and gave the guard a nod.

"What's your business in Cresience?" the guard demanded.

"Just delivering a message," Saim replied as he continued inside the gates. He did not get far, for the guard placed his hand on Saim's shoulder.

"One last thing, traveler."

Saim turned to the guard, almost positive of what was to come next. The man pinched the back of the hood and pulled it to lay on Saim's shoulders. Nodding with satisfaction, the guard could see that pointed ears were not poking out from Saim's long hair. Even if he had pulled his hair back, the guard would have only seen the poor, mangled excuse Saim had for ears.

"Sorry about that," the guard laughed. "Just had to be certain. Don't want one of those long-eared demons in."

Saim nodded with a scowl on his face, pulled his hood back over his head, and continued to lead the horse into the arched gateway.

Inside, the kingdom was scattered with an array of many humans. Some sold flowers, spices, fruits, vegetables, and different meats from small carts along the road while other people looked through their goods. All the sellers shouted claims of having the best products for the lowest price, while beggars caked in dirt and wearing shredded rags pleaded with the shoppers for any spare coin.

Saim reached the front of The Pewter Flagon, and tied the horse to the post near the trough using another knot he had learned at some point as a child. Yet another distant memory buried deep in years of hardships.

"Stay here," Saim grumbled to the horse, while stroking her mane. "I'll be back for you."

She leaned into his hand and let out a little groan. He would never know it, but she hoped this wouldn't be the last time she saw him. However, her instincts led her to believe this was a false hope as he left her side, and walked into the front doors of the tavern.

Instantly, his senses were overwhelmed by the sour smell of ale and wine, the sound of the lute played by the bard in the corner, and the quiet chatter of the few patrons enjoying their beverages at the tables. Standing behind the bar, Micah handed a flagon of ale to a man as he slid him a coin. After picking up the specie, Micah looked up to see Saim approach.

"What can I get you—" Micah began, but stopped himself and smirked as he recognized this hooded individual. "Oh, Saim. What brings you here?"

Saim took a deep breath before uttering, "It's about your father."

"Is that right? And what's the old codger done this time?"

"He's dead."

Micah looked up from wiping down the bar and glared at Saim, who was unable to make eye contact with what was sure to be an emotional reaction. It wasn't that Saim was insensitive, but the half-elf had never felt a bond with someone deep enough to know loss of this magnitude.

Micah turned to the bard and slammed his fist down while shouting, "Enough music!"

Surprised, everyone in the tavern turned to the bar, and the bard's fingers stumbled over the strings of the lute before he stopped plucking the old tune. Stumbling to his feet, the bard ran up to Micah's side behind the bar with lute in hand. Holding onto the bard's shoulder, he whispered something into his ear, and like a bolt of sky fury, the bard was out the tavern door.

Finally, Micah turned to Saim and asked, "How did it happen?"

"I found him in his bedroom after this morning's chores."

"I didn't ask how you found him," Micah grumbled. "I asked how it happened."

Saim shook his head. "I'm not certain. He had been there for a while. Looks as if he had been drinking."

"Poisoned."

"It's possible."

Micah took a deep breath, and cleared his throat as he pulled a bottle of wine from behind the counter. After pulling the cork on the bottle, he tilted it toward Saim to offer him a drink.

Saim held up his fingers in a polite refusal. It was just that he preferred a dark ale to fermented grapes.

Micah shrugged, took a drink from the bottle, and after swallowing said, "You know, when I last spoke to my father, he was preparing for this day. Who would get his possessions, and what not."

Saim watched Micah take another large drink from the bottle without breaking eye contact.

After a gulp, Micah continued, "When I asked about his farm, do you know what he told me?"

Saim shook his head.

"He told me that he was to give it to you," growled Micah as his face melted into a grimace. "He said that I had made my life in Cresience, but you. You had nothing. Nothing but loyalty. He said you earned his farm."

Saim was speechless. He had spent all his time at Gormah's farm tiptoeing around his employer's temper, so the mere thought of inheriting anything but a tongue-lashing from him seemed implausible. It was as unexpected as lightning on a day without clouds.

"Don't look so shocked, Saim," mumbled Micah, "because I know this couldn't be that unexpected."

Saim looked into his eyes with confusion.

"Yes," Micah whispered as he leaned in, "I think you knew. And I think you poisoned my father."

He stepped back with a smirk, but Saim continued to glare at him, puzzled.

"Guards!" Micah exclaimed as he pointed to the half-elf, "it's this one."

Suddenly, Saim felt the grip of two men's hands on both of his arms, and after a panicked glance to his sides, he saw two of Cresience's guards determined to subdue him.

"Careful," warned Micah, "he's got the blood of an elf in his veins."

Saim pulled one of his arms free, and reached for the barkeep. But before he could get him in his grasp, one of the guards pulled his sword, and after raising it over his head, he brought the bottom of the hilt down firmly on the nape of Saim's neck. He dropped to his knees in a daze only to be met with the hilt again. This time on his temple, and everything went black.

...

Staying out of suspicion was easy for the stranger, who had been staying in Cresience ever since Saim had begun working at Gormah's farm. And before that, he used his charm to find Saim as the half-elf traveled from place to place, finding odd jobs to get by. In the shadows, from afar, and hoping he would never have to interfere, the stranger watched and waited for this day to come.

The door leading to The Pewter Flagon flew open, and he watched as two of the kingdom's guards carried Saim's unconscious body out to their horse. Gormah's horse saw this as well, and with a worried neigh began to pull on the leather reins that bound her to the tying post. Realizing that this was futile, the horse reared back and began to kick at the post with her front hooves.

One of the guards carrying Saim turned to a group of three more guards, and barked the order, "Someone take care of that horse!"

The three guards ran to form a semi-circle around the front of the horse, grabbing the reins to keep her grounded, but she still kicked. The guards shouted with fear as they struggled to keep control of the creature.

The stranger would have been more concerned with the plight of the horse, but he was more focused on the guards throwing Saim over another horse with the Cresience crest hanging off of its saddle. After balancing his motionless body over the animal's muscular back, the guards led the horse down the road.

The stranger didn't have to follow to know where they were taking Saim. He was going to the dungeon, and if the guards knew he was a half-elf, his soul wouldn't be staying with him much longer.

...

In the darkness, Saim could only see a single red orb, and heard only breathing, but this was not his breath. Someone else was here.

"I know you have it, boy," uttered a deep, raspy voice, "and one way or another, I will take it."

Saim's body quivered in fear as the breathing and the orb came closer, allowing him to see the silhouette of the being, and discovering that the orb was one of its eyes shining in the dim light behind it. The figure towered over Saim, but after all, he was only a child.

"I will have the key!" the silhouette boomed as it grabbed the half-elf's small neck. "Even if I have to pull you apart to get it."

...

Saim's eyes snapped open from his nightmare, and he was instantly hit with a rush of pain shooting through his neck and face. He touched his temple gently, and groaned as even the slightest graze of his finger caused an excruciating sensation. This wasn't the worst way he had woken up, he though, but then he realized he was lying on the cold stone floor of a dungeon cell.

"I've been waiting for you to wake up."

Saim turned to the voice to see Micah sitting in a chair on the other side of the barred door.

"When my father told me that you would be getting his land, I was disappointed," Micah explained, "but when someone walked into my tavern asking if I had seen a half-elf, I was furious."

After sitting up with a groan, Saim rubbed his neck, wincing with every bit of pressure from his palm.

"If I wanted to hide my identity as an elf," continued Micah as he pointed to his own ear, "I would simply cut off that which identifies me. Just like you did. And I will die before I let an abomination have what should be mine."

"I didn't kill your father," Saim said between clinched teeth.

"Oh, I already know that."

Saim looked up at Micah, his head throbbing from the blow earlier and questions bouncing around inside his mind.

…

The dungeon guard sat at his desk outside the entrance to the cells, looking through a list of allegations against Saim. Usually, a trial would be held by the general of Cresience's army, but the most serious offense on the list was that a half-elf penetrated the walls of the kingdom, and that bypassed the right to judgment. The second page of the allegations was an order of execution to be signed by the dungeon guard. The criminal was to be hanged by the neck at first light. This was not to be a public execution, because if the people of Cresience were to find out how easily a half-elf got in, a panic would stir through the streets that could bring the hard stone buildings to a burning rubble by week's end.

Just as the guard signed the order of execution, the stranger walked through the door leading to the outside. The guard looked up as he folded the document, picked up a lit candle on the desk nearby, and dripped the melted wax on the paper.

"Can I help you?" the guard asked as he picked up the stamp and pressed it firmly into the wax to seal the document.

"I've come to see the prisoner just brought in," replied the stranger.

"Sorry, only one visitor at a time."

"I see," said the stranger as he grabbed the coin purse from his belt and tossed it on the desk. "Perhaps I could persuade you to let me in."

The guard looked down at the pouch with a scowl, and shook his head.

"I was hoping you wouldn't say that," sighed the stranger as he picked up his coin pouch, reattached it to his belt, and in one swift motion, unattached his sword and sheath.

With another quick movement, the guard unaware, the stranger swung the sword still inside its sheath. Surprised, the guard attempted to stand, but the flat side of the sheath caught the guard on the side of his face and he fell to the ground, out cold.

...

There was a thud from the guard room on the other side of the dungeon door, but Saim's attention was still on Micah, who sneered as stood.

"You see, Saim, my father was a lush," Micah began. "I knew that, because every week I would send him more wine."

Suddenly, it all became clear. Saim's eyes widened as the realization of the horrible deed Micah had done sunk into his stomach like a jagged blade.

The half-elf whispered, "You killed him."

Satisfied, the barkeep turned to the guard's door, and pounded on it to signal that he was done. After a moment, the sound of jingling keys could be heard on the other side, then the unlocking of the door.

"Fare thee well, abomination," Micah gloated. But before he could have another thought, the door flew open and struck him down to the cold dungeon floor.

The stranger walked into the dungeon wearing the helmet and tunic of the Cresience guard, and before Saim knew what happened, planted a dagger into the back of the barkeep.

Micah groaned, "Why?" as the stranger pulled his sword from his sheath.

Leaning down, the disguised man placed his blade against the barkeep's throat and grumbled, "A man of your valor deserves not another breath."

A quick jerk of his wrist, a splash of crimson on the face of the stranger, and Micah went limp on the stone floor.

Saim had not moved, blinked, or breathed. His head still throbbed and the heavy beating of his heart didn't help. However, his discomfort was not what troubled him. It was the sights just on the other side of the bars as the stranger turned to him, and removed the guard's helmet.

The half-elf knew this man, but he had changed since they last spoke. Wrinkles now cradled his eyes, and gray streaks had found their way into his brown beard and hair, which was now at shoulder length. It was a man whom Saim had once had the chance to kill, and now the half-elf wondered if he should have taken that chance as the man placed the guard's key in the cell lock.

"Come boy," Havish said as he opened the jail door. "It's time to leave this place."

Chapter III

"**W**ell?" Havish asked as he held open the cell door, "What are you waiting for?"

Saim glared at him, from the cold, stone, and dirty dungeon floor, motionless and puzzled. Nothing could have prepared him for the events he had lived this day, and he remained still with his mouth agape.

"We have to go, boy," Havish said as he stepped into the cell. "We don't have much time."

He reached for Saim, but just before touching him, the half-elf scooted himself against the uneven stone wall while shouting, "Don't touch me!"

"Damn you, child!" Havish exclaimed as he took a few steps, and lifted Saim by his shirt. "Do you want to find your end, or will you put your misguided faith in me for just a few moments, so I can save your short life?"

Saim looked into Havish's eyes, desperately searching for a shred of sincerity. Saim would truly die in this kingdom's dungeon, but gambling his freedom with this human could end the same way. But wait - panic and tears in the bard's eyes? Was that the sincerity the half-elf was looking for? Perhaps a gamble would be the best option. After all, it seemed to work for Saim's mother.

...

Following a night of travel, the sun had begun to peer over the horizon, casting tall, dark shadows from the trees in the thick forest. Saim watched his mother, Lurya, speaking to Havish. His mother told him to stand at a distance while she and the human spoke. While he couldn't hear what they were saying, the tears in Lurya's eyes told a story of despair. This gave the small half-elf a chill that could be felt from his toes to the pointed tips of his ears.

Havish leaned toward Lurya, but she placed a hand on his chest. He stopped, reached up to her face, and wiped her tears away. She finally nodded, walked to her child, and knelt down to meet his concerned gaze.

"This man is Havish," she started with a quivering voice. "I want you to listen to everything he says."

Realizing the situation, tears welled in the child's eyes as he whimpered, "I want to stay with you."

Saim's words shook the tears from his mother's eyes, and she replied, "You can't, my love. It's not safe."

The half-elf's knees became weak, and his body shook with a sadness that tested all of his willpower to remain on his feet. Lurya pulled him close in an embrace that was so tight that it seemed to squeeze the tears from both of them.

The drops soaked into the clothing on both of their shoulders, and the elf whispered into her son's ear, "I love you."

Young Saim's mouth opened to say that he loved her too, but all his voice could muster was a staccatoed whimper. Lurya released the child, stood, and walked back over to Havish. They too embraced for a moment, and after a few more words, Havish walked over to Saim.

"Child," Havish mumbled, holding out his hand, "we had best be going."

The half-elf took the bard's hand, and was led to his nearby wagon, but not once did Saim take his eyes off of his mother. She waved, doing everything in her power to dam the tears overpowering her eyes. As Havish lifted the boy onto the front of the wagon, Saim saw her wipe them away.

The human climbed in the wagon as well, and with one guttural shout and a whip of the reins, the horse began to move forward. Soft sobs escaped from Saim's mouth as he and the bard moved down the path, and Lurya shrunk in the distance as she stood watching her son leave.

The half-elf's eyes began to hurt from glaring at the silhouette of his mother with the brightening sun rising behind her. Saim finally looked away for a moment to rub his eyes, and when he looked back the wagon had moved over a hill. He could no longer see her, but when he blinked his eyes he could still see her figure, so young Saim kept his eyes shut until the figure faded away a few minutes later, just like the years had faded the memory of her face.

...

The door leading to the dungeon slowly opened a crack, and Havish's eye looked out into the guard's room. He saw the unconscious guard laying on the ground, but nothing else had changed since he had last been in the room.

Before he moved any further, he put the Cresience helmet back on his head, turned to Saim, and ordered him to take the dagger from the barkeep's back.

The half-elf looked over to Micah's twitching and blood-soaked corpse, and grimaced at the thought of pulling the blade from the lifeless body.

"Hurry," whispered Havish. "'Tis only a dead body. I can guarantee this will not be the last we come upon, and certainly not the last I'll create."

Saim moved to the body, and slowly reached out to move it. Wincing the entire time, the half-elf lost a bit of his innocence as he nudged the body over, and wrapped his hand around the hilt of the dagger. He quickly pulled on the handle, but the blade didn't budge, and instead slightly lifted the corpse off the ground. This caused the half-elf's stomach to turn, and a cold sweat to coat his body.

"Get on with it, boy," Havish hissed.

Saim furrowed his brow at the bard, then took a deep breath as his gaze went back to the cooling body. With a groan, he planted his foot into Micah's back, and pulled the blade free past the scraping bone. He swallowed the bile rising in the back of his throat, and slung the blood off of the dagger onto the floor. Then he wiped the weapon on the clean part of the corpse's shirt.

Saim and Havish met eyes, and nodded at each other. Then the bard opened the door to the guard room, leading the way by taking the first steps into the room. With the half-elf following close behind, Havish grabbed a pair of shackles hanging on the wall.

"Tuck that dagger into your pants," Havish said as he tossed the shackles to Saim. "And put those on."

Saim looked at the shackles with confusion, and back at the human.

"I can't very well just take a prisoner without binding his hands, can I?" asked Havish.

The half-elf sighed, hesitantly hid the dagger in the waist of his pants, and fastened the iron shackles loosely on his wrists in front of his body. Meanwhile, the human grabbed the sealed document off the guard's desk.

"What is that?" Saim inquired.

"My boy," Havish replied as he presented the paper, "you were to be executed by this letter. And now, it is a means for your freedom."

The half-elf was nervous. He could understand the plan, but it still didn't calm him to know the order of execution was in the hands of a human, whom he trusted less than a rodent alone with a loaf of bread. However, this was the risk he knew he had to take.

"Off we go," announced Havish as he got behind Saim, and nudged him to the door.

Saim inched toward the door leading outside, and with a deep breath, pushed through.

Instantly, the half-elf was blinded by the daylight, which sent a dull throb of pain through his already-aching head. By the position of the sun, he guessed he had been out for most of the afternoon. If he had been at Gormah's farm, he would be prepping the old man's supper, so that he would be finished eating once the sun went down. Saim would have been eating what was left soon after that.

Havish led the half-elf to the archway leading into the marketplace, which was guarded by two members of the Cresience army. Saim held his breath to compose himself, but the bard remained confident and firm in his ruse.

They walked past the guards, but after the third step from the archway, they stopped as a guard spoke up with, "Halt!"

Havish turned slowly to the guard, but Saim remained facing away to hide his fear.

"Where are you taking that prisoner?" asked one of the guards.

"I have orders to take him to the gallows for execution," the bard replied without pause.

"I have not heard of an execution today," said the other guard.

"The order is here," Havish announced, holding up the sealed letter. "It is to be brought with haste to the general waiting at the gallows."

"Let me see that," ordered the first guard while the second placed his hand on the hilt of the sword sheathed on his belt.

Saim began to instantly perspire, and his legs shook as he fought the urge to retreat. But Havish stayed sure-footed and straight-faced.

"I'd be happy to let you see it," began the bard, "but I doubt the general would appreciate the seal being broken on an order to be delivered to his hands first."

The guards looked at each other with concern, and finally turned back to Havish.

"Very well," sighed the first guard as the second lowered his hand from the hilt of his blade.

With a smile, the bard turned, and nudged Saim forward. The half-elf sighed with relief, but the tension returned to his body when one of the guards shouted, "Wait!"

Havish turned to him again, but this time inched his hand toward the handle of his weapon. Saim too grabbed the dagger tucked into his pants.

"Gallows are the other direction," laughed the first guard.

This time with a much bigger grin on the bard's face than before, he responded, "Of course. I do not know what I was thinking."

Havish gripped the half-elf's shoulder, spun him in the opposite direction, and began to lead. Through the archway, out of the corner of his eye, the bard noticed a man stumbling out of guard room with a dazed look on his face, and a bleeding bruise on the side of his face. A guard without a tunic or helmet. He locked eyes with Havish.

"Kill those men!" ordered the dungeon guard, and without hesitation, the guards at the archway pulled their swords.

The bard acted with a speed the likes of which Saim had never seen. Havish held up his sheathed sword, blocking the swing of one of the guards. Then in one motion, he used the guard's blade to hold his sheath in place as he pulled his sword free. Using the momentum, the bard swung the blade across the torso of the other guard, who instantly fell while trying to hold in his vitals. Havish carried through with his swing, and nearly took the head off of the first guard.

As the bard regained his footing and the archway guards became corpses at his boots, he didn't have time to react to the dungeon guard running toward him. Saim, as if by reflex, threw down the shackles on his wrists, pulled his dagger from his waistband, and buried it in the dungeon guard's neck, stopping his sprint cold. The half-elf stared into the guard's eyes as they rolled back into his head, and pulled the blade free, letting the body fall into the pooling blood.

Saim and Havish looked at the several shocked faces of the marketplace patrons as Havish grumbled, "I hoped for less bloodshed on this endeavor."

"After them!" shouted someone in the distance.

The bard and the half-elf looked to the source of the shout, and saw five members of Cresience army heading through the marketplace crowd to the scene of violence.

To this Havish exclaimed, "Run!" and darted to the opposite direction.

After a glance at the lifeless dungeon guard, Saim followed. He had never killed a man before, and perhaps later he could reflect on that. As for now, he could only escape with his life.

The bard pushed through some people in the crowd, and rushed down an alley headed toward the residential district. The half-elf, with his years of farm work, had no problem hopping over the fallen market patrons and keeping up with Havish.

Suddenly, two soldiers appeared at the opening of the alleyway with swords drawn. As one swung the sword, the bard ducked, letting the blade strike the stone wall of the alley. He planted his shoulder into the soldier's stomach, and they both fell to the ground. As Havish straddled the member of the Cresience army and planted his blade into his chest, the other soldier lifted his blade over his head to strike. Saim grabbed his tunic and swung him with all his might into the nearby stone wall.

Havish and the half-elf stood over the writhing bodies of the two soldiers, but couldn't celebrate their victory for long as they noticed a couple of Cresience's horsemen in the distance headed toward them.

"With haste, Saim!" cried Havish as he headed to the kingdom entrance.

As they both hurried to the wall archway, the horses came closer and closer.

"We cannot flee on foot!" Saim shouted.

"Just a little farther!" announced Havish.

They crossed under the archway, and Saim instantly saw the unconscious entrance guard, Gormah's horse, and another steed just outside the wall. The bard instantly hoisted himself on his horse, and the half-elf climbed atop Gormah's.

"To the forest!" Havish commanded.

With a kick in the side, the horses darted toward the woods with Saim and his protector on their backs, but the Cresience horsemen were not far behind. The horsemen were gaining ground on them as they approached the treeline of the forest.

"Duck!" Havish yelled.

The half-elf lowered himself on the back of Gormah's horse, and the bard did the same, but he raised his sword and cut a rope near the entrance of the forest. With a high-pitched *whoosh*, a tree limb whipped over the heads of the horses, and struck Cresience's horsemen across the face, causing them to fall off their horses.

Saim and Havish looked back at the fallen horsemen, whose horses were now running aimlessly away from them.

"We have to keep moving," the bard began. "They will be searching for us through the night."

"You planned all this?" asked the half-elf in disbelief.

"I did," Havish answered as he stared ahead to dodge the trees going by. "For you."

"Why?"

"Saim, you are more important than you realize."

Chapter IV

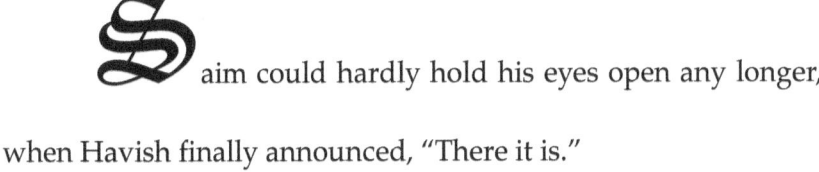aim could hardly hold his eyes open any longer, when Havish finally announced, "There it is."

After an entire night of riding, a small farming town approached on the horizon. The homes and shops looked black in the morning sun, and the half-elf had trouble focusing on them. His muscles ached, his head throbbed, and the confusion of the previous day still swam in his mind. Conversation would have helped Saim stay focused, but Havish had not spoken since they left Cresience. Any question the half-elf came up with was met with a promise of an explanation later.

There were only a few people on the roads, and the rest were in the fields tending to their crops. Saim was surprised to see entire families working together, instead of one person doing all the work.

One patron stood out among the rest of the townspeople; he was much shorter than the humans, stout as a barrel of ale, and a scent to match. Saim had never seen a dwarf in person. He also didn't know how to read, but after comparing pictures he'd seen in books to the one before him, he could see that the artists were fairly accurate in their depiction.

The dwarf's long red hair was tangled in his beard with beads holding strands out of his eyes and keeping his mane away from the leather straps across his chest. Attached to those straps, a harness containing a large steel hammer. Blocky and brass designs on the hammer matched the armor on the dwarf's chest and shoulders.

However, the dwarf seemed more intimidating, because of the beast attached to the reins gripped in his thick fist. Wearing similar armor on its head and ribs, the boar stood at least twelve hands tall with tusks the size of a man's lower leg. The saddle on its back indicated that this was a means of travel for the stocky warrior.

Saim's eyes sprung open as the dwarf raised his voice to a human nearby, "You'll regret it, you miserly whelp!"

"If you don't want the same treatment, avoid his eyes," advised Havish.

But it was too late. The dwarf turned his gaze to Saim, and bellowed, "And how about you fine gentlemen? Surely a couple of weary travelers are in need of my services."

"Sorry, friend," sighed the bard. "We are in no need of a guide this day."

"A guide?" The gruff fellow laughed as he walked along the side of their horses with his boar in toe. "You insult me."

"We mean no insult," Havish said.

"I will forgive your trespass, for you know not who I am," the dwarf explained. "Allow me to enlighten you. I am Rust, and my companion here is Porter."

Rust motioned to the boar, who snorted as if to introduce himself.

"I fight for any that can afford my superior skill set," he boasted.

"It's nice to meet you, Rust," Havish began. "However, all our coin will be tied up in supplies for our journey."

"I implore you to reevaluate your expenses," said Rust. "The wood surrounding this town can be treacherous, even more so at night. Furthermore—"

"Again," Havish interrupted, "I apologize, but we cannot afford your guardianship."

The dwarf furrowed his brow, and stopped in his tracks to push his words from the depths of his belly. "Keep your apology for when you face the snarling monsters in the forest. Then you will truly be sorry."

Rust's shouting continued with Porter's groaning as Saim and Havish rode farther away. Even though it was clear his rant was being ignored, he didn't stop until another person crossed his path. Then a synonymous self-promotion rang out over the fields, until he was out of earshot.

It wasn't much longer until Havish dismounted his horse in front of a small shop and tied the reins to a post just outside the doors. Saim followed suit, and accompanied the bard in-side.

The interior of the shop was illuminated with candles and sunlight from the windows, giving just enough light for the merchant behind the counter to spot thieves sneaking goods into their pockets.

"Welcome," greeted the shop keep. "Hopefully, that cave dweller outside didn't give you too much trouble."

"Worry not, my good man," Havish chimed as he app-roached the counter.

As the bard went through pleasantries with the merchant, picking out the items needed for their travels, Saim found himself mesmerized by the soft glow of the candlelight reflecting off of the different weapons behind the shop keep: long, short, blunt, pointed, a few two-handed, some common, some with decorated hilts, and some with unique blades. But one weapon in particular caught the half-elf's eye. It wasn't decorated, but it was functional. Just a modest long bow.

...

When Saim had reached his twelfth year, he found that someone his age could no longer rely on the sympathies of people to be given coin for food. It was early in the morning, and he decided this was the day he would find other means to feed himself.

His first attempt at hunting found him covered by the leaves of a tree as he sat on one of the thick branches, waiting for an animal to come by. After only a small shift of the sun, he began to doze off from boredom and the warmth of the daylight. His body went limp, and he leaned to the side, almost falling out of the tree. He managed to snap awake, and catch himself before losing his balance.

Saim would have sighed with relief, but he noticed a corpulent rabbit hopping near the trunk of the tree. His mouth instantly salivated at the thought of tasting the tender, cooked meat. Maybe he could make a stew. Maybe he could find a way to dry it out and ration it for a week. Or maybe he would just eat it all, until he was so full that he would have to sleep it off.

After quietly perching himself on the branch, Saim was ready to pounce. He took a deep breath, never taking his eyes off of the prey. His stomach moaned with anticipation. Finally, he was ready to claim his prize, and he leaped from the tree.

Saim fell with his arms out, but didn't account for the other tree limbs around him, and one hit him hard in the shoulder. This spun him around and caused him to land with a thud on his back. Trying to catch his breath, Saim remained on the ground groaning in agony. He turned his head to see the rabbit in his reach, but it scampered away as he made a futile attempt to grab it. The young half-elf remained there for several moments, thinking of a new way to capture breakfast and waiting for the pain to subside.

The sun moved across the sky a bit more, and he was back in the tree. This time, he used some rope he found in the stable to make a trap, and a crust of bread he had saved to lure what would be now be his lunch. Then he saw it, the same varmint that caused him so much pain earlier. Revenge was at hand, and hunger was on the way out.

The rabbit approached the bread circled by the rope dangling from the half-elf's hands. The animal nervously smelled the air, eyes twitching in all directions to make sure it was alone. A hop closer. Another hop. And another. With a final leap, the rabbit was in the trap.

Saim pulled with all his might, but this again made him off-balance. He waved his arms back and forth to stay on the branch, but the angle at which he was leaning made this hopeless. On the way down, he continued flapping his arms as if he would be able to slow his fall. A groan escaped his throat when he met the ground once more. Out of the corner of his eye, he spotted the hare near him. He swung his hand desperately to catch the animal, but it was gone in a flash.

After one more trip to the stable, Saim managed to steal a flat, wooden pitchfork. Armed with a weapon, he was ready to finish this vendetta once and for all. Staying low in the heavy brush of the forest, he searched for the rabbit that managed to make him look foolish twice. Other animals crossed his path, but he was much too focused on finding his vengeance.

The sun moved farther across the sky. The young half-elf's stomach ached with hunger, his body was sore from the falls he had taken, and fatigue caused him to quake. He was on the verge of giving up, and going back into town to beg for coin when he finally saw the fat bastard grazing on some leaves.

Saim slowly crawled through the tall grass careful not to make a noise, but an unseen twig found its way under his knee, and it snapped under his weight. The young elf stopped, and kept his eyes fixed on the rabbit. It looked up from its meal, and glanced around.

Saim held his breath.

Finally, the hare seemed to decide it was safe and continued eating, so the half-elf inched closer. In no time, he was close enough to spear the animal, so he sprung up from the brush with the pitchfork over his head, and brought it down with all his twelve-year-old might.

The hare darted, barely evading the pitchfork. Saim pulled the points free of the soft dirt and ran after the rabbit. He thrust the pitchfork down over and over again, but the animal was much too quick.

Saim was so focused on killing it, he didn't notice he was headed for a steep hill. The hare stopped at the edge, facing the young half-elf. But when he lunged his weapon forward, the rabbit darted between his legs.

The twelve-year-old attempted to pull the pitchfork free, and spin for another strike, but he instead fell forward, sending himself and his hunting tool tumbling down the hill.

At the bottom, among all the bruises he was sure to earn, Saim felt a sharp pain shoot through his thigh. He sat up to see one of the long, thin pieces of the broken pitchfork stuck in his leg. He let out a shriek as he pulled the point out of his bleeding wound. It wasn't as deep as he thought it would be, but this would still slow him.

At that moment, he noticed the narrow, long shape of the sharp, pointed piece of wood. This gave him a silly, desperate, and rather impractical idea.

As the sun went down, young Saim collected the rope he had used earlier, and found a slightly curved branch he had knocked to the ground on his second fall from the tree. Then he secured the rope tightly on each end of the branch. When he plucked the rope with his finger, it made a low, almost musical tone. It was a crude bow with an even cruder arrow.

Finding another tree to conceal himself in, and using some of the leaves he had seen the hare feasting on before as a lure, he waited for an animal to appear underneath his hiding place.

At the first shine of moonlight, a rabbit came up to the trap to fill his belly with the leaves. Saim realized it wasn't the same one he had held quite a grudge against, but he was famished. His rumbling stomach outmatched the volume of his head's cry for revenge.

The half-elf pulled in enough air to fill his lungs, and held it in as he brought back the narrow piece of wood on the taut rope with his index and middle fingers. The curved branch arched more, and Saim used his finger to line the projectile up with the creature's head. His form was perfect, but he could only hope his weapon would hold up. As the branch's fibers began to crackle, he slowly let the air loose from his lungs, and released the rope.

The broken wood slid across the curved branch and Saim's finger, breaking a splinter off into his flesh. With the sound of wind around the arrow as it sped the short distance to the rabbit, it met the target. Maybe not with the accuracy Saim intended, but it still impaled the hare's side.

The young half-elf's finger bled from the splinter, but he was too happy to care about the pain. He threw his make-shift bow over his shoulder and climbed down the tree as quickly as he could. His victorious cheering could be heard all through the forest, until he finally looked at his prey.

The animal shivered, gasped for breath, and stared into Saim's eyes with a look of fear he had never seen before. This was the first time he had ever taken a life. He picked up the rabbit, careful not to inflict more pain on its pierced side, and instantly began to weep as he heard a quiet whimper.

Saim never considered the pain he would inflict. For a moment, he related to the small animal. Too little to fight back against the ones that hurt him so, and now he was nearing the end. It wasn't graceful, or dignified. It was terrifying, and agonizing.

Saim came to the conclusion that he must help this being. It was too late to save it, but perhaps the right time to assist it in moving on.

"I'm sorry," the young half-elf whispered.

Using all his remaining strength to hold the hare by his head, he slammed it against the tree trunk. The lifeless rabbit lay limply in Saim's hand as he wiped away his tears. He placed the body on the ground, and while continuing to mourn for the innocent life he took, he collected the items necessary to build a fire.

...

Havish finished listing the things they would need for their travels, and as the merchant turned his back to retrieve it all, the bard noticed what his companion was looking at.

Havish added, "I'll also take a quiver of arrows, and that bow as well."

Saim looked over at him, surprised, but the bard just smiled, and placed his pouch of gold on the counter.

It was only a few moments before they left the shop, and were headed out of the small town on their horses. As they neared the woods, Saim felt the weight of the arrows on his back and the bow over his shoulder. Havish had also bought him new clothes. Among the shirt, pants, and boots, he had a new leather-armored vest.

As they neared the thick treeline of the approaching forest, the half-elf's confusion was so heavy, he demanded an explanation from his benefactor by asking, "Why are you doing this?"

Havish smirked and replied, "You need to be ready for whatever danger may come."

"What danger?"

"As I said, Saim, you are special, and I am not the only one who knows this. That's why I've been watching you for all these years, keeping you safe."

"From whom?"

Before Havish could answer, a screech was heard echoing through leaves and branches above. They both glared up, trying to see what would make such an alarming noise, but only a shadow blocked the light for a moment as it flew over the treetops. Saim thought this sound was familiar, but he couldn't distinguish it.

The ground rumbled as the trees in the distance shook violently. Something had landed, and was headed their way. The horses both stopped in their tracks and let out a neigh as if begging to retreat, but Saim and Havish were frozen in fear. A tree fell to the side as the creature marched closer. Every step shook the earth, until it finally showed itself, using its claws to swipe down the last oak in its path.

The winged, black dragon stood on all fours, taller than a horse. Upon its back was a man wearing the clothes of a swashbuckler: tall boots, a dirty shirt, and pants to match. He pulled a thick curved blade and patted the scaled, horned beast on the back of its head.

With that, the dragon reared its skull back, bringing it back down to blow a line of fire blocking the way forward. The swashbuckler leaped off the dragon's back, avoiding the fire, and landed in front of Saim's and Havish's horses.

A toothless grin crossed his face as he said, "Unless you fancy becoming a pile of smoldering ash, the half-breed comes with me."

Chapter V

Havish's fingers inched toward his sword in his belt, but the swashbuckler could see this and shouted, "If ya think I be bluffin', pull your blade, and Ember here will make sure you never doubt my word again, bard."

The dragon, Ember, stood behind the burning brush, and let out a grunt to agree with his handler. The smell of sulfur lingered in the air.

Havish brought his hand up in surrender, but smirked calmly, and said, "By the look of you, I should have known better. I apologize. But I must know, a man of your intellect mustn't be taking orders from a pirate. I mean—"

"Your silver tongue will not delay things," the man interrupted. "He comes with me."

Saim remained motionless atop Gormah's horse. The bard managed to get him out of trouble once, so rather than flee, he decided to trust in the man who had seemed to protect him his whole life.

"So you're not interested in a silver tongue," uttered Havish. "Perhaps a pouch of gold can sway your loyalty?"

The swashbuckler wet his lips, as if the sound of a hefty bribe made him salivate. But it was clear he chose to remain loyal to whomever employed him, as a scowl slowly washed over his face.

"My allegiance is with Captain Separ," he uttered.

Captain Separ was a name Saim had heard before, both in legends, and whispered by his mother in curse.

...

Both Lurya and her newborn were exhausted from the birth. The child had been cleaned up by the ship's apothecary, a man who had experimented with rare ingredients most people shied away from. As the infant was placed into his mother's arms, she instantly fell in love with him, even though she knew it was possible that no one else would accept him. The gentle swaying of the large vessel rocked the babe to a peaceful slumber, and Lurya was soon to join him.

Her eyes were heavy, and her head began to droop. One thought kept her mind uneasy as she looked at her child's beautiful face. Right now, he hadn't a care in the world, but he would know of the world's bigotry one day. Neither the elves or the humans would accept him, but what really troubled Saim's mother was who the newborn's father was.

"Where's the newest member of my crew?" asked Captain Separ as he entered the apothecary's quarters.

He was a human, who seemed to tower over everyone, and his broad shoulders could barely fit into most doorways. The weight of his steps caused the ship's wooden floors to groan under his boots. His skin was bronzed from the sun glaring down on the deck of the large boat, and the top of his bald head was red from the bright and clear sky.

He rarely wore a shirt due to the heat, and this day was no different. The skin of his torso and arms stretched across his strong features, and was covered in inked pictures of dragons, fire, and ancient texts. What wasn't covered in black marks was occupied by scars from previous battles. A few of those scars were deep gashes on his face, partly covered by an eye patch. And the wounds that caused them would have killed lesser men, but to Separ, they were lessons in how to kill more efficiently.

As the captain's eyes rested upon the newborn, a smile broke through his hardened face as he exclaimed, "Finally, a treasure too priceless to part with!"

As he laughed deep from his belly, Lurya put her finger to her lips and whispered, "He's sleeping."

"Now is not the time for rest," Separ began as he reached for the babe. "It is a time for celebration!"

Lurya tried to keep the child in her arms, but she realized that her hesitation was futile. The small half-elf began to squirm and sob as he was cradled in the captain's thick arms.

"You're upsetting him," the elf woman said.

Separ ignored Lurya as he glared at the infant with pride, uttering, "I need to introduce you to the rest of the men."

The captain rushed out of the door with the newborn, and the elf woman stumbled to her feet, weak from giving birth, trying to stop him. She leaned against the doorway, calling out to Separ to stop him, but it was too late. He was headed up the stairs to show the rest of the crew his new treasure.

The child's eyes ached as they adjusted to the bright sun, causing his cries to almost drown out the chatter among the pirates working on the deck, the growling of the ten dragons caged at the stern of the ship, and the soft splashing of the open sea's waves on the sides of the vessel.

With the babe in his arms, the captain stomped up the nearby steps to the bridge of the ship and shouted, "Men! Gather round and hear me!"

The pirates, even the ones feeding leftover meats to the dragons behind Separ, turned their attention to their captain.

"Behold," he announced, presenting the crying child over his head, "the boy has come! Our new shipmate! My seed!"

The crewmen cheered for the new father, and with a sneer on his face Separ held his offspring out in front of him to stare into his eyes. Confused by all the noise, the infant went silent, meeting the man's gaze.

"We are one and the same," the captain grumbled.

And from that point on, Saim was what they called him.

...

"Surrender the half-elf," ordered the swashbuckler. "Now!"

Havish glanced back and forth between Saim, the man, and Ember still standing behind the flames.

"Have it your way," said the swashbuckler as he turned to his dragon. "Ember—"

"Wait!" the half-elf cried, "I'll go with you."

Even Saim couldn't explain why he suddenly cared about the well-being of the bard, but he figured Havish had saved his life once by helping him escape Cresience; perhaps he could do it again. If not, the half-elf still owed him for that.

"Saim," the bard warned, "no."

"We don't have a choice," the half-elf mumbled as he dismounted Gormah's horse.

"Leave your weapons," commanded the pirate.

Saim glared at the man with disdain, and finally sighed, nodded, and took off the bow and quiver of arrows. After throwing them on the dirt, the half-elf walked to the side of the swashbuckler, exchanging worried glances with the bard.

"I can't let you do this," Havish uttered with desperation.

"You don't have a choice," said the pirate as he pulled a pair of shackles from his belt.

"Please," pleaded the bard, "I'll give you anything. My gold. My steed. My life. Anything."

"That won't be necessary," grumbled the swashbuckler while locking the shackles on Saim's wrists, "because I'll be taking all of that anyway."

The half-elf and Havish's eyes widened with panic.

"Ember," called out the pirate, "kill him."

The dragon reared its head back, and let out a roar deep from its belly as it stretched its gigantic wings. Daylight shone through the thin skin, showing every vein and bone. The bard could only marvel at what he was sure would be the last thing he would see before he was burned alive.

Suddenly, the crash of falling trees echoed in the woods, which silenced everyone, including Ember. Before they could turn their attention to the source of the sound, a colossal boar broke through the nearby brush with a dwarf holding a war hammer over his head. Rust's and Porter's mouths were both open wide in a triumphant battle cry.

With everyone distracted, Saim took the opportunity to ram the swashbuckler with his shoulder, causing the man to fall into the cracking flame.

The boar slammed his tusks into Ember with a force that threw Rust off his back and over the burning grass.

After falling on its side, the dragon scrambled to its feet, took a deep breath, and shot a line of fire at Porter. But the boar easily sidestepped the attack, and with one quick thrust, gored Ember deep in the chest. The dragon let out a howl, and collapsed lifeless on its side.

Rust slid on the ground as he landed, and spun to face the pirate, who stood up out of the flame. The pirate began to pat out the fire on his shirt, and with a growl of frustration, raised his sword to strike Saim. Before he could swing his blade, the dwarf struck the side of the swashbuckler's head with his ample hammer.

The pirate moaned on the ground with a crimson pool forming around his split skull. Only one of his wide open eyes seemed to still function.

With a sigh, Rust stood over the dying man, raised his mighty hammer over his head, and brought it down on his face with such a force that it spotted everything close to it with red.

The forest had never been quieter. The only sounds that could be heard was the dwarf's heavy breaths and Porter kicking dirt up to put out the flames.

"I don't want to insult your intelligence," huffed Rust, "but everyone knows you don't make deals with pirates."

Dumbfounded, Saim whispered, "You saved us?"

"Ah, this one speaks," laughed the dwarf. "Back in town, I had you pegged for a mute."

"How?" asked Havish. "How did you know? Why did you save us?"

"Full of questions, but not a tinge of gratitude," replied Rust. "Perhaps you'll find some thanks after some supper?"

Porter's ears perked up, and he stopped kicking dirt on the fire.

"Good thinking, Porter," praised the dwarf. "We'll need a good fire to make something to eat."

"We are grateful for your aid, but we only have enough supplies for ourselves," Havish said.

"Oh, I have all I need right here," Rust laughed as he patted Ember's corpse. "We'll be eating dragon tonight. Meanwhile, you and I can discuss payment for my services. Seeing how you two have fared on your travels so far, I can tell you'll need all the help you can get."

Chapter VI

"**So**," began Rust as he swallowed the still-bloody dragon meat he was chewing on, "where are we going?"

Havish, Saim, Porter, and the dwarf sat around the fire that had been started by the dragon, now roasting in pieces over the flame. Nearby their horses stood quietly, resting from the attack with bellies full of the oats purchased in the town earlier that day.

The sun was still in the sky, but a lot of time had passed as Rust waited for his fresh kill to cook. Due to a dragon's natural resistance to high temperatures, it still had the texture of a freshly slaughtered cow. This was why Saim and Havish preferred the salted pork from their saddle bags.

"We haven't agreed that you're going with us," the bard grunted before he bit into his piece of salted pork.

After tearing the last bit of meat from the leg bone he held, Rust threw it to the eager boar laying beside him and laughed, "We may not have spoke the words yet, but we know the outcome of them."

"How am I to know you didn't set up this ambush, so that we would hire you?" accused Havish.

The dwarf furrowed his brow, and squinted into the bard's gaze, uttering, "If I were willing to kill only for your money, I would already have it. Now wouldn't I?"

Rust and Havish glared at each other for a while, until Saim broke the silence with, "The dwarf brings up a good question. Where are we going?"

The bard broke his stare with Rust to look at Saim, but his expression of frustration lingered.

"You haven't even told the boy where he's going?" asked Rust. "Glad to see your inability to trust didn't come from meeting me."

Havish turned back, his temper held back by a weak emotional dam trembling at the pressure as he said, "We can't afford to pay you now, but you will be compensated for your loyalty if you can promise it."

After licking his stubby fingers clean and wiping the bloody remnants of Ember's hardly-cooked flesh on his pants, Rust extended his stout hand toward the bard. With a sigh and a look of hesitation to Saim, Havish reluctantly grabbed hold of the dwarf's forearm, and gave it a firm shake.

With that, the bard sat back, looked at everyone, took a deep breath, and explained where they were going.

...

The war had been waged for generations. Kingdoms fell, villages leveled, and forests burned. Lives were lost, kings were dethroned, and yet no victory was reached by either the elves or the humans.

Dwarves were no better than the humans in the eyes of an elf, because they too were far too concerned with technology, and were hollowing out the underground in search of the materials to create their inventions.

The only solution to end the chaos was the complete separation from one another. Humans and dwarves stayed in towns, kingdoms, and mining colonies. Elves buried themselves far within the thick woods of the continents, constructing elaborate and beautiful settlements with nature to protect them from the elements, dwarves, and humans alike.

Naughstaure was the one of the most well-known elven colonies, but had been seen by so few people, some doubted it existed at all. The only way to get to Naughstaure was through a dense forest, which was home to creatures that were a danger to anyone that stumbled upon them. The only things certain of Naughstaure was that the travel there would mean death, and if you were anything other than an elf, arriving there would mean the same thing.

...

After explaining the destination, Havish demanded they got on their way, so they extinguished their fire, mounted their beasts, and continued through the lush wood. The whole while, Rust sang old dwarven war songs. After a glance at Havish's annoyed expression, Saim smiled for the first time in years.

"In the dank, dark hole

they crawl to us in vain.

For we swing our blade,

their blood, a warm rain.

From the Abyss they rise.

And our mines they fall.

The soulless, foul assault

ends when we call...

  In death you give us purpose.

  In life you give us pride.

  We'll fight till our bones are broken,

  and our bodies finally die."

It was a song that described an age when the dwarves had banded together to take back their several mines from evil creatures known as abysmyths. They were often thin, but oddly strong, and their skin was black with cracks showing their lava-like blood pumping through their veins. Sharp claws and a lack of reason, these monsters appeared one day from the mines dug by previous dwarves. Suddenly, cave-ins and strange mutilations were an every-day occurrence, but the dwarves fought back. They drove the abysmyths back into the depths never to be seen again. A triumphant moment deserved a triumphant song.

Before Rust could go from the chorus onto the next verse, Havish groaned, "Enough. Please."

"A bard stifling song," Rust scoffed. "Now that I can't believe."

"It's not the song I wish to stop," replied Havish. "It's the silence I wish to start. We have already been taken off-guard once, and I wish to not attract more attention."

The dwarf sighed, "You're the employer," and he stayed silent for only a few moments before humming the tune to himself.

"Rust!" the bard exclaimed. "Please!"

Porter groaned in defense of his rider, but after patting the large boar on the back of the head, Rust whispered, "Easy. He's a bard without song. He has a right to be frustrated."

Saim could feel the tension grow as he watched the scowl grow more prominent on Havish's face. so he decided to intervene with the question, "Were you in the war with the abysmyths, Rust?"

"No, I was much too young," answered the dwarf, "but I have faced a few of them in my time."

"Impossible," mumbled the bard.

"Is that so?" Rust challenged. "Maybe you have another explanation for the scars on my body."

"The abysmyths have not been seen since the elves helped the dwarves drive their forces away," Havish explained.

"You bards always think you have the whole story," the dwarf said.

"I am a traveling bard," corrected Havish. "It is my responsibility to get information from the bards in each settlement. Bards are a part of a brotherhood, of which we have no secrets. We gather both stories of legends and history."

"Human history," groaned Rust.

"Is that how you were able to keep track of me all these years?" Saim asked Havish.

The bard turned to the half-elf with a smile and proudly announced, "Finally, someone gives me evidence of an intelligent thought."

...

Havish awoke. He did this, like he did every day since young Saim came into his care. His head aching and stomach churning from the overindulgence of wine the night before, he wiped the sleep from his eyes with a groan. Sunlight made his pupils shrink, like stone doors slowly grinding shut in his sockets.

"Saim," the hungover bard moaned, "it's time to wake up."

Everything finally came into focus in the blue hue of the rising sun. The smoldering logs of the night's fire, his horse, and his wagon was all that was around him. Saim was nowhere to be seen.

Havish sprung to his feet in a panic shouting, "Saim?"

Had the young half-elf been taken in the night? With that thought, the bard reached for the dagger in his belt, but only felt an empty sheath.

He cursed himself for imbibing in the wine so heavily the night before, but how else was he to cause a child so much pain by trimming his ears? A sober man would never be able to do such a horrid task, even if it was for the child's own good. The humans would never let a half-elf walk among them, and it was imperative that attention never be brought to Saim.

The child must have run away, and the bard had to figure out where he would have gone to. With that thought in motion, Havish mounted his wagon and led his horse to pull him to the nearest town.

It only took a small fraction of the morning to get to a small settlement that would have taken a small child the day to reach on foot.

Havish rode his horse up to the closest tavern, but this time not to drown his sorrows in a strong beverage. For a bard, there was no better place to find information than a place that served ale. One taste of the fool's drink, and people were willing to share anything with a charming enough fellow.

After tying his horse to a post, he headed inside the tavern. The smell of stale wood, fresh spirits and beer, the sound of laughter and conversation flooded his senses. However, Havish was listening for the soft lute and gentle song of the bard in the corner of the room. It was a song of lost lives during the time of war with the elves. It fell on deaf ears of the bloodthirsty humans, even though it was written by one long ago. Some people would sing the song because of its infectious tune, but most had no idea what it meant.

The tavern bard ended his song with little applause following, but even though he thanked them for the low level of enthusiasm, Havish could see his frustration.

"Brilliant song," Havish said while approaching the tavern bard. "And it was performed very well."

"My thanks, friend," he replied.

The bards grasped each other's forearms, and gave them a firm shake. This meeting eventually took them to a table with a couple of tankards of ale between them, and Havish wasted no time asking if there were any stories of a child with bandaged ears being seen around the town. Just so happens, he had. Apparently, the orphanage picked him up, because they felt sorry for the unfortunate child walking about with his ears slashed.

That meant maiming the boy had worked, even though it pained Havish so to do it. Saim fit in among the humans, and he was safe.

For days the small half-elf's protector camped in the woods near the settlement debating with himself whether or not to interfere in the child's life any further. True, he had made a promise to Lurya that the boy would be safe by his side, but it was possible that away from him, the child could live a life without fear from the pirate that wanted to end it.

Meanwhile, Havish would be in the shadows, hidden in the crowds, watching Saim grow, learn to hunt, and struggle into adulthood by himself. Or rather, it would seem that he was by himself.

Havish's choice was a hard one to make, but he stuck by his decision. That was, of course, until he got word of a pirate asking the now-deceased Micah if he knew of a man matching Saim's description. Havish had paid the bard working at The Pewter Flagon to alert him the moment Saim was in danger, and that's just what the bard did the day the members of the Cresience guards took him to their kingdom's dungeon.

Moments later the half-elf's protector would bring him back his freedom, and they could begin their trek to Naughstaure.

...

The night had come, so the travelers sat in the dark eating on the meats from their packs. It was difficult to see in the dim moonlight, but a fire would give away their position. Though Rust had no issues with this, because his race was known for their superior vision even without light. As for the others, they would have to sacrifice their sight for the time being.

"We should reach Naughstaure in a day's travel," explained Havish, "but we must rise early to make it through the forest outside its walls. Those woods are not a place to make camp."

With a grunt, Rust nodded in agreement, but Saim still had questions, "Why are we going there? What are we running from? Or to?"

Havish sighed and announced, "We should get some sleep as soon as we can."

"What's all the secrecy for?" Rust scoffed. "Shouldn't the boy know why we are going through the most dangerous forest on this continent? I'd like to."

"I don't want to give too much of the plan away, until I know we are not being followed."

"And if we die before then?" uttered Saim.

With a sigh, Havish responded with, "I suppose you're right. The man after us—"

"Wait," interrupted Rust. "You claim to be a bard, but I have yet to actually see any proof of that."

"And?" Havish groaned.

"I'd like a bit of showmanship," mumbled the dwarf.

Havish smirked, reached into his pack, and pulled out a small flute. He placed his fingers over some of the holes on top, but before putting it to his lips, he explained, "I'm out of practice, and I can't see where my fingers are, so keep that in mind."

And with that, the bard inhaled, placed the flute in his mouth, and began to play a haunting melody, introducing the story of the ruthless pirate Captain Separ. The Dragon Voice.

...

A few more moon cycles had passed since Separ had taken control of the dragons, and the young elven woman he saved from being sacrificed for the Eye of Sight Unseen had stayed by his side ever since. Although he did hate her race for what they almost did to him, Separ refused to kill elves ever again, because he had fallen deeply in love with one. Her name was Lurya, and she lived only because he rescued her.

Lurya couldn't return to the elves, because in their eyes she had betrayed them for not allowing her life to be given on the altar. Separ left a life of bloodshed behind, and this too made him a traitor to his race. But with the dragons under his control, no one would dare cross him. This was eventually what ended the war.

Free and with nothing to fear, the elf and the Dragon Voice assembled a crew, and set sail in search of their fortune. Lurya had heard the stories of what powers the Eye of Sight Unseen had from the moment she was chosen for sacrifice. Yes the orb allowed one to control the dragons, but this was not its only purpose. It was able to hear and speak to the beasts. It was how the dragons received commands from the one who had it in ownership, but it was also able to tell the keeper the location of a key, and the location of a door for the key to unlock.

Behind this door was a mystery. Legend claimed it is a treasure so priceless, the one to claim it would be the most powerful being alive. As outcasts of their own people, the Dragon Voice and the elf woman craved that power. They could take it by force with their winged creatures, but ruling by force was not enough to satisfy them. Lurya and Separ wanted their people to not oppose their rule, but to beg for it.

Of course, with great power, it's quite difficult to know who you can trust. One night, the Captain had caught a member of his crew attempting to steal the Eye. He was so angry he put the man to death on the spot. From that moment on, he never trusted another soul. The paranoia drove him mad, until one day he decided to find a way to ensure the Eye would always be with him.

In a fit of rage, he cut out his own eye to replace it with the orb. This struck fear into all who knew him, including Lurya. He had become what he had sworn he wouldn't. A man who leads with fear.

When the elf woman realized she was pregnant with Saim, she knew the child would not be safe in the company of the Dragon Voice. Not only because he had become a pirate under the delusion he could trust no one, but because the Eye had begun to reveal to him that the key to opening the door leading to the treasure of ultimate power was to show great sacrifice. To a father, no sacrifice is greater than his own son.

...

The bard finished his story with a few notes from his flute, which was followed by silence. Saim was speechless.

The only thing he could think to ask in all the quiet was, "Is it true?"

"Yes, boy," replied Havish. "Separ is your father."

Rust nodded his head, saying, "A half-elf? That must not make you too popular."

Again, Saim didn't know what to say.

"And a father to consider killing his own child?" grunted the dwarf. "Does any man have that heinousness in his heart?"

"I have no doubt," said the bard as he glared into the night sky. "He's already killed the child's mother."

Chapter VII

$\mathfrak{J}$t was a day filled with travel that began the moment the sun touched the sky with its morning hue, just as Havish had planned. As he, Saim, and Rust rode upon their mounts, they remained silent. Other than the occasional dwarven tune, no one could think of a topic to dull the painful truths the half-elf had heard the night before.

The sun was in its final movements across the sky as they finally cleared a set of hills and found themselves at the treeline of the forest leading to Naughstaure. As if by instinct, everyone came to a stop and stared into the thick woods. Saim's troubling thoughts silenced to allow him to hear only the sound of the wind pushing through the foliage. Not even the chatter of birds reached his deformed ears.

"We're here," whispered Havish.

As if to hide the fact that he was intimidated by the forests legend, Rust pointed out the obvious. "It's quiet."

The horses and Porter exchanged glances grunting to confirm that even though they had never heard the legends, they too felt something wrong with this place. Something very worrisome indeed.

After a deep breath to cleanse the concern from his body, Havish kicked his steed's side, saying, "We haven't much daylight left, and I shudder at the thought of navigating these woods without the aid of the sun."

With that, the bard entered the treeline. Reluctant, yet in agreement that darkness would only make things more treacherous, Rust and Saim followed Havish into the unknown.

It took only moments of travel before they were surrounded by thick brush and trees with no sight of land outside the forest. It was the point of no return, and only the sun could tell them which direction they were heading. But the light was becoming dim.

"We should go back," warned Rust.

"No," Havish began. "It's too late for that. We press on."

"How are we to get our bearings without light to guide us?" the dwarf demanded. "Soon we won't be able to see a blasted thing at all."

"There is only one direction to go," explained the bard. "Forward."

A sour look came over Rust's face as he looked to Saim for his correspondence, but the half-elf only looked forward with no expression.

At this point, maybe death was the best possible outcome for Saim. Better to die with the dangers that waited ahead than to die at the hands of his murderous pirate father. At least then Separ couldn't have whatever treasure lay behind that lost and mysterious door.

Small droplets of water began to seep through the treetops. The smell of moisture in the air, although a good sign for the farmers of the land, was only another bad omen for the travelers as they drudged on. A flash of bright, white light and the sound of nature's fury boomed suddenly, making everyone gasp out of surprise.

Havish caught his breath, and whispered, "It may seem as though we will lose our guiding light early, so step lightly. Keep your voices down. The weather may help us remain undetected, but let us not test our fortune."

"Our fortune?" scoffed Rust.

Soon the rain began to beat down on their shoulders, thunder tested their ears' constitution, and the lack of sunlight obstructed their vision with only few moments of lightning to show their path.

The dwarf could see much better than his fellow travelers, but due to large gusts of wind, the whole forest swayed disguising any movement of possible dangers.

Finally, they reached some sort of landmark. A tree taller than any seen since entering the woods, and thicker than half the towers man had made in all the kingdoms. They paused their journey for a moment to marvel at the natural giant. Even Saim gape at it in awe.

"We're halfway there," Havish informed. "Not much longer now."

So onward they went, and the farther the trek, the heavier the steps of their mounts became as their hooves sunk into the softened dirt. The wood was quickly turning into a marsh.

Without warning, an explosion of energy burst through the sky and struck one of the taller trees in front of them. With a hard tug on the reins, everyone stopped in their tracks, staring at the glowing embers in the wound of the tree trunk. Over the sound of the rain, a cracking could be heard. Havish's eyes widened as the sound became louder, and the branches tilted toward him.

"Back!" the bard cried as he turned his steed to run in the opposite direction.

Porter didn't wait for Rust to give him the command to get away from the falling tree, and quickly followed Havish's lead. Saim tried to escape, but when he yanked the reins of Gormah's horse, she reared back, throwing the half-elf to the ground, then ran off into the darkness of the forest.

Saim choked as the air in his lungs was forced out from the contact with the ground. The branches coming closer and closer, a groan was all he could seem to muster as he slipped on the mud trying to maneuver out of the way.

With a deafening *thud*, the tree struck the ground inches from the half-elf's face. Both Havish and Rust dismounted their beasts, and ran to Saim's aid. He would have sighed with relief if he wasn't busy gasping for breath.

"Are you hurt?" the bard asked as he knelt over him.

Saim shook his head, but couldn't say anything through the coughing.

"He's fine," laughed Rust. "He just got the wind pulled from his sails. That's all."

Havish got to his feet and looked in the direction of where Saim's mount ran, and pondered aloud, "What got into her?"

"Can you blame her?" chuckled Rust. "It's not every day a tree makes an attempt on your life."

Saim turned and finally managed to take in some air. Then he noticed something out of the ordinary. The remaining horse stood on a puddle, but seemed to have trouble remaining still. Its hooves slowly seeped deeper into the mud, and it began to whine with uncertainty.

The puddle bubbled near the horse as something slowly began rising from the muck. A head and shoulders? The being continued to rise from the earth, until it had become a mound as tall as a man. From the shoulders, mud collected to form two appendages over some fallen branches that were stuck to it.

Still choking on his breath, Saim couldn't make any noise that would warrant alarm. He continued to gasp for air as a flash of lightning struck through the clouds above, and what he saw quickly put fear into his heart.

An elven skull emerged from the center of the monster's head. The jaw swung ajar as if screaming, but only a hissing gurgle was heard.

The horse began to plea for its life, but out of fear and lack of breath, Saim could not call attention to the horror. It walked toward the half-elf, its foot falling apart and reforming with every step, and held out one of its arms. Sharp twigs and rocks came to the surface of the creature's arm, creating a crude, spiked club, raising it overhead for an attack. Saim tried to stand but couldn't find the friction to lift himself.

It seemed to be the end of the half-elf's journey, until Rust's hammer split the creature into only a stomach-high pile of wet earth. Old bones and twigs were left poking through the top of the mud as the muck climbed up the broken pieces, carrying more bits of wood and bone to repair itself.

Before Saim could finish watching the creature pull back together, Rust grabbed his hood and lifted him to his feet crying, "To arms!"

The half-elf looked around to see another one of the creatures heading toward Havish, who was pulling his sword from the sheath, and another monster forming from the mud nearby. He turned back to face the being next to him, just in time to see the muck pull the elven skull back onto its shoulders.

"I'll take care of this one!" shouted Rust. "Help the bard!"

As Rust swung the hammer at his foe, Saim took the bow from around his shoulder and pulled an arrow from his quiver. Havish had his hands full with a creature, but the newly formed monster was closing in as it pushed a tiger's skull through its shoulders to form its head.

Saim nocked the arrow and let it loose. It flew past the bard and struck the mud beast in its torso. This only seemed to get its attention as the arrow stuck into its surface and slowly sunk down to the ground.

The half-elf launched another arrow at the creature, but it quickly melted into the earth below. Confused by its actions, Saim lowered his aim. He suddenly felt the ground bubble at his feet, and he spun to see what was happening just in time to see the tiger skull directly in front of his face. It was attached to a tall pillar of wet earth that was also holding Saim's ankles into place. Arms were starting to form from the muck, and there was no way for the half-elf to move away.

Saim gripped the end of his bow and swung it as a blunt weapon. The bow sunk deep in the monster and wouldn't come out. The half-elf pulled on his bow with all his might, but it was hopeless.

The creature hissed and wrapped its undeveloped limbs around Saim. No matter how much he fought, the mud seemed to keep engulfing him, pinning his arms to his sides.

Finally, the half-elf was forced to his back and felt the earth swallowing him. He turned to Havish, Rust, and Porter to scream for help, but they too were overwhelmed and being devoured by the mud. Their arms flailed, and their defeated cries were silenced by the muck covering their mouths, turning their shouts into a dirty foam.

His mouth filled with the mud, and the need for air was well past due. His vision began to darken and blur as life crept from his body. Even though Saim welcomed death before, it was in that very moment he changed his mind. Maybe it was best for him to live. He might live his entire life in fear of Separ at his heels, and he would always be an outcast. Whatever life it would be, he wanted it.

As the wet earth crept to his eyes, he saw a flash of bright white light. Soon after, he felt the mud harden, as if the moisture had been pulled from it. Cracks made their way through the creature, and it began to crumble. Was it dying? Were they being rescued? Saim's eyes felt too heavy to keep open, and he wondered if assistance came too late.

In his last conscious moment, he thought he saw Gormah's horse approaching from the woods. And something was on her back. Someone. A woman. An elf. If he didn't know better, he could have sworn it was his mother.

Chapter VIII

Late one night, young Saim woke in his mother's chamber to find that Lurya had left his side. He wasn't sure how long she had been away, but because she had never left his side from the moment of his birth, it was very out of the ordinary. Then again it had only been a few weeks since they were forced to move out of the Captain's quarters, so maybe this was another change he would have to get used to.

Just then, the door flew open, and Separ walked in pulling Lurya by the hair behind him. He threw her down on the wooden floorboards, pulled a dagger from his belt, and knelt over her. After grabbing her hair by the roots, he pulled her head back to face him, and held the knife to her neck.

The young half-elf could see the blood running from the corner of his mother's mouth as she whispered, "Please."

"Tell me where you were?" Separ grumbled.

"I just needed some fresh air," Lurya whimpered with tears in her eyes.

"You left the ship!" he shouted.

Separ, crazy with paranoia, demanded his crew remain on the ship, even when docked. His men felt as if it was a prison sentence, but their captain had proven time and time again that the consequences for disobeying him was a punishment that ensured they wouldn't do it again. The punishment was death, after a lengthy and painful interrogation. No one dared leave the ship, but the elf woman had a greater purpose than to be a lush in the port taverns. She was trying to save her son.

"I just needed a drink," she lied.

"We have spirits on board!" Separ shouted as he pressed the dagger into her neck, causing a small trickle of blood to run down to her collar bone.

Young Saim had finally had enough of this violence, and he leapt off the bed. He screamed running toward the Captain, but he was much too small to do any harm to a man, let alone a man the size of Separ.

The captain grabbed the half-elf and slammed him on the floorboards. Then still holding the blade to Lurya's neck, he used his other gigantic hand to both pin and squeeze the child's neck.

"Lie to me again, and I will choke the life out of him!" threatened Separ.

Pain was shooting through Saim's body, but the pressure on his throat was beginning to tighten. His lungs began to burn, and his eyes felt like they were about to pop from his sockets.

"He's your son!" Lurya screamed. "You can't!"

The Captain ignored her, and asked again, "Where were you?"

She looked at her child's face gasping for breath, and back at Separ. If she didn't tell the truth, it could mean the death of her and her son. But by telling the pirate that she left to speak to a bard she had met years before, so that she could arrange for him to take young Saim and hide him from the captain; she would certainly be executed, and once the door to the treasure was found, her son would still die.

"We only have ale and rum," she bluffed. "I just wanted to taste wine again."

Separ glared at her, watching her eyes for a tell. Then finally, he loosened his grip on Saim's neck, and sheathed his dagger saying, "I'll arrange for wine to be brought on board."

With relief washing over her, Lurya sighed, "Thank you."

"Do not take this mercy as a sign of weakness," the pirate captain groaned as he stood, and walked to the door. "You have my word that if you leave again, my men will have to clean your blood from every board of this vessel."

97

She nodded, and Separ left the room. The young half-elf jumped into her arms as they cried away the fact that they were so close to death. The child didn't understand what it all meant then, but Lurya knew that in only a few days her son would be far away from all this.

...

The creaking of wood and tightened ropes was all that could be heard in the darkness. Saim was alive, but it was difficult to open his heavy eyelids. Light finally made its way into his vision, and he could see that Rust and Havish were with him inside a cage made of wood and vines hanging high above the ground. The dwarf paced impatiently as the bard sat somberly in a corner.

From inside his captivity he could see an extravagant kingdom. All the mammoth trees and rocks had been hollowed out, constructed into homes and castles. Fireflies, glowing vines, and floating orbs provided enough light to see every detail. Adult, child, elderly, male, and female elves all walked the organic pathways wearing elaborate clothing made from earth-toned fabrics. It was surely a sight to behold. It was Naughstaure.

"They saved us," Havish informed, "Dried up the mud-golems, and brought us here."

"Straight to this cage," grumbled Rust. "Been here ever since."

Saim slowly got to his feet to look upon the land he thought he would never see, and he could not find words to express his wonder.

The only words to escape the half-elf's mouth were, "We made it."

Far below, two elves could be seen approaching the tree from where the cage was hanging. One had a crown on his head made from golden leaves; the other was a woman wearing a long robe made from light green and brown cloth. In her hand, was a mage's staff crafted from wood. At the top was a translucent jewel that began to glow green.

With a wave of the mage's staff, the branch the cage hung from began to groan and crack. Saim held onto the wooden bars as the cage began to lower, but before he could panic about falling from the great height, he noticed they weren't dangling from a tree at all. He noticed a face, legs, and arms of flesh in the bark. The giant creature of wood and gray skin slowly lowered the three captives to the ground. The cage landed softly, and the two elves stood face-to-face with Saim.

The male elf stood tall and slender with a look of authority. His long brown hair rested perfectly on his shoulders, and his yellow irises seemed to stare through the Saim. Beside him, the mage posed, hugging her staff. Her black hair and olive skin set off her green eyes, which glared at the captives with disappointment. Despite her lack of approval, and the scar on her left cheek, she was beautiful.

"I am Faylin," said the male elf in a deep tone, "and you should thank the Great Spirit that Maurna here was able to find you in time."

"Great Spirit?" scoffed Rust as he walked up to the bars in front of the elves. "Release us from this cage, you pointy-eared devils."

Maurna raised her staff to the dwarf, shouting, "You do not speak to our king that way, underling!"

Faylin grabbed Maurna's shoulder, giving her the order, "Calm your temper. These travelers know not who I am."

"I don't care who you are! Where is Porter?" shouted Rust.

The mage turned to her king and spoke to him in her elven tongue angrily, but Faylin remained tranquil as he responded. This was when Havish finally stood and approached the bars near them, and also said something in elvish as well.

Faylin turned to the bard with an impressed smirk, mumbling, "You know Elvish. Interesting."

Maurna too seemed taken aback from the human speaking their native tongue.

"Your horses and boar are safe," the king informed them. "They are resting in our stables with all your belongings. We will take you to them."

Faylin turned to the mage and gave her a nod. With a sigh, she touched her staff to the wooden cage, and the bars bent to provide an exit.

"My thanks for your understanding," said Havish as he stepped out of the cage.

Rust pushed Saim to the side, grunting, "If Porter is hurt, I will burn this kingdom to the ground."

Saim saw Maurna furrow her brow at the dwarf as he passed her, and he tried to calm her down by saying, "He's just very protective of his mount."

"You should be too," mumbled the mage. "Your horse saved your life."

The half-elf was confused by this statement, but he stayed quiet as they walked through the kingdom to the stables.

On the ground, the trees seemed to reach into the heavens far from sight. The people looked happy. This was an uncommon sight for Saim, who grew up around humans.

Finally, they reached the stables inside of a hollowed tree. Their mounts seemed in better care than they were. Large piles of golden hay filled the room, soft leaves provided beds for whatever creature wanted to rest, and troughs overflowed with a vegetable stew that the elves considered slop. But with the way Porter had his snout buried in it, it was a gourmet feast.

The boar noticed Rust walk in out of the corner of his eye and immediately stopped eating to run to his side. Careful not to hurt the dwarf with his massive tusks, Porter pressed his head against him.

Wiping the food off the boar's snout, the dwarf said, "It doesn't seem like you missed me too much, but it's good to see you, too."

Gormah's horse walked away from the elf brushing her mane, and rested her head on Saim's shoulder. Confused by the steed's sudden loyalty, the half-elf patted her neck.

"Why'd you run away, girl?" asked Saim.

"She didn't run away," Havish explained. "She came here to ask for their help. Elves can communicate with all beings in nature."

The half-elf was astonished by this, but had to admit he too always felt a certain relationship among all living things. However, he never understood it until now.

"Even I knew that," laughed the dwarf. "Some half-elf you are."

The bard turned his eyes angrily toward Rust, and the elves gasped out of shock. The dwarf bit his bottom lip, causing his mouth to disappear into his thick red beard. He had realized the mistake he made, and so did Saim as he placed his palm on his forehead.

"A half-elf?" exclaimed the mage.

"Not so loud," commanded Faylin.

Yet, Maurna still shouted, "He's an abomination! He must be dealt with!"

"He's Lurya's son," informed Havish, "and he's what Separ needs to open the Door of Sight Unseen."

Faylin and the mage gaped at each other with a look of concern. They knew the legend well, but never thought their lives would intertwine with it.

Finally, the king said, "We must take you before the Elders."

...

It's true that possession of the Eye of Sight Unseen drove the pirate captain to the edge of sanity, but what pushed Separ to an unbending psychosis was the night he carved out his own left eye and replaced it with the orb. The moment the wound began to heal around the jewel, he started to hear voices. It was the twisted thoughts of the dragons, and foul monsters known as the abysmyths.

Elves were able to understand all things natural. However, they had never been able to speak with the winged scaly creatures. Through careful observation and legend, elves learned that the thoughts of dragons traveled through a dimension simply called the Abyss.

At the time before war raged between races, an elven mage, a human scholar, and a dwarf with great knowledge of runes and precious jewels created a small window into the Abyss entrapped in an orb. They called it the Eye of Sight Unseen.

Able to listen and command the thoughts of the dragons, it was a great tool that removed the threat of fire-breathing beasts attacking dwarven mining colonies near their nests to the north and south, but also allowed humans and elves alike to tame the beasts for air travel. Unfortunately, the Eye came with a problem. The dragons spoke through the Abyss, but this other plane of existence was also where the most vile of all beings dwelled. The home of the abysmyths.

It was soon discovered that without the dragons at their nests, sightings of beasts made from fire, rock, and molten lava were reported. The dwarven mining colonies were the first attacked when they discovered a portal in the southern continent.

Only the dwarf, one of the makers of the Eye, could travel through the mystic portal with the help of the orb, but when he came back, he was changed. He was so enamored by what he found inside, he cut out his own tongue so he could keep the contents of the portal to himself. He died keeping the secret of his sights, only leaving behind a letter to his family saying the power it contained was too overwhelming for any one individual to have.

As the abysmyths' attacks spread to the human and elven settlements, it became a popular belief to the elves that the abysmyths were a creation by the Great Spirit as punishment for abusing the power of the Eye. The mage decreed that the orb was to be hidden away from the world, but the dwarves and humans had other opinions.

The dwarves needed the dragons gone to continue mining despite the attacks of the demons, and the humans had placed too much confidence in the transport of the dragons to further their people. Promises of war were on the shoulders of the Eye's remaining creators, but the blood of those slain by the abysmyths was on their hands.

Despite the new violence among their people, they hid the Eye deep in the dragons' nest in the Northern Continent. They burrowed deep, and created an altar of sacrifice in the heart of the volcano. If someone were able to take a life in order to obtain the orb, the watch of the dragons would surely stop them from getting the Eye of Sight Unseen.

Knowing that possession of the orb allowed one to physically travel through the portal, they created a second altar and a stone door that would require a great sacrifice to use. They called the large, unmovable stone gate the Door of Sight Unseen, and with the price of its use too high, no one would dare attempt to open it.

That was until Separ managed to get his hands on the Eye, and by placing the orb in his bleeding socket, he allowed a direct line for the abysmyths to tempt him. And one night, as he slept, finally able to ignore the many thoughts of the dragons, the Eye gave him a vision. The secret to opening the door buried deep in the Southern Continent.

He awoke from his slumber in a cold sweat, and barely able to breathe, Separ whispered, "My son."

...

The six elven Elders were the oldest living among the rest of Naughstaure. While explaining the legend of the Eye of Sight Unseen, they all spoke in a unified whisper. They were the teachers of the Great Spirit, and to become one of them meant sacrificing their individuality. Though they were still separate bodies, they all shared one mind and one voice. They stayed in the main tower carved from the thickest, largest tree in the natural kingdom away from all distractions, never leaving the chapel. Even if they wanted to abandon the thrones, their flesh had become part of the tree that they remained inside. This would be a prison sentence to a dwarf or human, but to an elf, there was no greater honor.

Saim, Havish, Rust, Faylin, and Maurna stood before the Elders as they finished their history lesson, waiting to see if they had any more to say. Even though their whispers ended, they continued to echo in the large room.

"My Elders," began the king, "what are we to do with the half-elf?"

A breath was heard, as if the wood they were inside was pushing air into the ancient elves' lungs, and they explained, "The Great Spirit finds all life, even that of an abomination, sacred. So he should be only cast out to find his way through the dreaded forest."

"Your word be done," said Faylin with a bow of his head.

Saim, Havish, and Rust sighed with relief as the mage grimaced in disappointment.

"However," the Elders uttered, "this is a case of different circumstances."

Maurna picked her head up as a smirk crossed her face.

"If this Separ were to gain control of this half-elf's life, it would mean chaos. The end of this world," continued the whispers.

"Pardon my insolence," Havish started before Maurna raised her staff to silence him.

"How dare you address the Elders!" she shouted.

"Let the human speak!" boomed the voices.

Maurna shook with anger as she lowered her staff, and nodded to Havish to let him know he could continue.

"I brought Saim here in hopes that he could be kept safe," explained the bard. "Separ wouldn't dare storm the gates of Naughstaure."

"And if he does?" pondered the Elders.

"Then you can stop him," Havish advised as he walked up to them. "Your army nearly wiped out all of our strongholds during the war."

"This is true," agreed the whispers, "but the war was long ago, and our military is untrained and not prepared for battle."

The bard fell to his knees at the Elders' feet, and pleaded, "I beg you. I promised his mother I would keep him safe."

A tear fell from each eye of the old elves as they looked upon the human in pity. Maurna and Faylin had never seen the Elders so affected.

"Your words move us, human. And we understand your plight," consoled the voices. "But the risk is too high. And we cannot afford the bloodshed."

Havish lowered his head in defeat, and after a sigh, he whimpered, "Then we'll leave. We'll find elsewhere to hide."

"You and the dwarf may leave," the whispers began, "but we cannot allow the half-elf to leave here alive."

Saim's jaw dropped in shock as he said under his breath, "No."

"You can't!" yelled the bard, jumping to his feet. "I won't let you!"

"I'm sorry, human," the Elders expressed gently. "You do not have a choice."

Havish leapt on the elevated platform where the ancient elves sat, but before he could take a step farther, the Elders raised their heads, and thick vines fell from the ceiling, wrapping around the bard. As it lifted him screaming in the air, Rust attempted to run for the door. But Maurna quickly struck the dwarf in the back of the head, knocking him out cold.

Saim was frozen in fear, and as Havish continued to scream obscenities, all sound became muffled in the half-elf's ears. The only thing he could hear clearly was the voice of the elven king as he approached him with a saddened look on his face.

"I am sorry, young one," Faylin mumbled as vines sprung from the ground, binding the half-elf's hands and feet.

Chapter IX

Faylin sat at his desk in his chambers, glaring at the flame atop a nearby candle.

He was deep in thought, just as Maurna walked in through the archway, informing him, "The prisoners are secured in the cell, my lord."

The king took a deep breath, preparing to give the most controversial order he had ever given. It wasn't illogical, but perhaps unreasonable, considering that the decree of the Elders was usually treated as the word of the Great Spirit itself.

"It's not a solution," mumbled Faylin. "It's only temporary."

"My Lord?" Maurna asked, puzzled.

"To kill this half-elf," the king began, "it will not solve the problem. It only prolongs the inevitable."

"I don't understand."

Faylin stood from his chair, and walked closer to the mage, saying, "This Saim is the key to Separ, because it is his son. If that which is most precious is destroyed, it would only leave a hole to be filled at another time. Another sacrifice. A man holds more than one thing above all else, and losing one only makes the next thing in line that much more sacred. It makes something else the key."

The mage began to understand, but she reminded the king, "He is an abomination."

"The true word of the Great Spirit is to love all that which lives," Faylin explained. "Be that plant, animal, man, woman, child, elf, or dwarf. These things all live. Years ago, the war caused many of us to become bitter, but the Great Spirit forgives. The Great Spirit loves all that lives."

"You are talking about going against the orders of the Elders," scoffed Maurna. "Are you mad?"

"I am your king!" shouted Faylin. "And though the Elders are connected to the Great Spirit, they are still only elves."

"I did not mean to insult you," she apologized, "but you know the penalty for this."

"I do."

"Then what will you have me do?"

"While the kingdom sleeps, you are to release the prisoners, and take them to Runehelm." Faylin returned to his chair with a heavy heart and continued. "There you will acquire a ship, and travel to the Southern Continent. And you must find a way to close the Door of Sight Unseen forever."

"My Lord—"

"Separ must never open that door," he interrupted, "and no one ever shall be tempted to again."

The mage bowed her head to hide her tears and asked, "And what will you do?"

"I will stay," he grumbled through his quivering voice. "I will accept my fate."

With that, she wiped the tears from her eyes, and tried to come up with a way to talk him out of it. He was right, but she didn't want him to be. Hesitantly, she finally said, "As you wish, Faylin. My lord. My king. My love."

He gave her a nod while attempting to hide the sorrow, knowing this would be the last time they would see each other. She turned away as the strength of her tear ducts gave in to the overwhelming sadness. She managed to carry herself out of his chambers and down the hall, but before she could leave the tower made from a hollowed-out tree, she collapsed against the wall, slid to her knees, and sobbed.

She knew the elf who had raised her would be executed within days of her departure. She didn't want to do it, but not even the Great Spirit could talk her out of carrying out Faylin's last wishes.

Inside his chambers, Faylin picked up a wooden doll that Maurna had made for him when she was just a child. She had wanted it to look like him, but it came out looking like a small monster, yet he still loved it, praising her art. He held it against his chest as tears rolled down his face. And after a deep breath to compose himself, he put the doll in his pocket, walked out of his chambers, and went to the chapel of the Elders.

If he could distract them long enough, it would give Maurna enough time to leave unnoticed. Hopefully, never again would any elf in Naughstaure ever set eyes on her. This included himself.

...

It was late, still, and quiet as Saim found himself hanging in the cage high above Naughstaure once again. The kingdom had fallen asleep, and other than the occasional passing guard, the half-elf, Rust, and Havish were the only conscious beings in the kingdom, sitting on the wooden bars. Complete silence would have been achieved if it weren't for the bard's occasional apologies for failure to protect Saim, and the dwarf's taunts of cowardice for freezing up in fear.

"Your life is in the balance, and you do nothing about it?" criticized Rust as he rubbed the welt swelling on the back of his head.

"Enough!" Havish shouted. "That's not helping."

"I'm doing more than you are, bard," Rust complained. "Got any songs to get us out of this one?"

Saim had finally had enough of the bickering, and sighed, "Be quiet."

"You say something, abomination?" taunted the dwarf.

The half-elf turned to Rust with his face twisted up in anger as he slowly stood, commanding the dwarf, "Be quiet!"

Rust also rose to his feet and walked closer to Saim, asking, "And who is going to make me?"

The events prior to this moment flashed into the half-elf's mind, including the hardships he had to endure alone as a child. His life would have been a nightmare to even a diseased peasant, and he had always tried to remain thankful for what little he had. But he was to die by morning, and being humble just wasn't enough for him anymore. He looked into the approaching dwarf's face as the anger built up more and more.

Saim's fist seemed to clench on its own as he shouted, "I am going to die, and all you can think about is yourself!"

"I'm thinking about who will pay me when you're buried," replied Rust.

He would have said more, but the half-elf released all his fury to strike the dwarf down with a blow to his face.

Rust touched his throbbing jaw and, in shock, mumbled, "Where was that when we needed it?"

"I've got more," growled Saim as Havish sprung up, and held him back from further attacks.

"We are wasting time," the bard explained. "We need to find a way out of this."

"How?" questioned Rust while sitting up. "They have eyes in every inch of green in this place. It's hopeless, and you're the one that brought us here."

"You do not want another enemy in this cage," threatened Havish. "And as I recall, you are the one that said the term 'half-elf'."

Saim pushed the bard away, walked to the corner, and sat saying, "He's right. He's full of the same filth from the back side of a swine, but he's right about this. It *is* hopeless."

The bard and the dwarf looked to each other, realizing the half-elf's spirit was broken. Rust had no reason to keep berating him, and there was no use for Havish to even try to encourage him to keep going. It truly was hopeless in every way possible. Every way, but one.

Without warning, moaning wood and snapping twigs could be heard from the tree giant's arm as their cage was slowly lowered to the ground. They stumbled, trying to stand, glancing around quickly to see who, or what, was coming to their aid. No one could be seen anywhere in the darkness, and when the cage finally landed they still seemed to be alone.

That's when the sound of their weapons hitting the ground beside the cage almost caused them to leap through the wooden ceiling. Maurna, dressed from head to toe in wooden and stone armor, waved her staff over to the cell wall, and the bars opened.

"Keep your voices down, before you wake the entire kingdom," she whispered.

Between Saim, Rust, and Havish only the half-elf could think of something to say, even though it was only the word, "Why?"

"Be silent," she hissed. "And collect your things, so we can leave this place."

Not another word was said. They rushed out of the cage and to their arms. As soon as Saim secured the quiver of arrows to his back, they crouched low to the ground and followed the mage to a nearby tree. She peeked around the bark and motioned for everyone to hurry behind her.

After a moment of staring out into the distance, she waved her arm behind her to get everyone to follow. Without a sound they crept across a path and knelt down into some bushes, managing to get out of the line of sight of two guards walking down the trail past them.

Once the elves were out of sight, Maurna made haste to another tree. Havish and Rust hurried behind her, but as Saim moved away from one of the bushes, a twig brushed past the arrows in his quiver. Though it wasn't a loud noise, just a clicking as the projectiles shifted around. But on this quiet night, it might as well have been thunder.

Everyone froze to listen for footsteps, or conversation from approaching guards. All was silent, so the half-elf continued forward until he heard the elvish command to stop.

Everyone turned to see the two elven guards charging and pulling their thin blades from their sheaths. Rust, Havish, and Saim prepared their weapons for a fight, but before the half-elf could pull an arrow from his quiver, Maurna stepped forward and tilted her staff in the direction of the elves. The jewel on top glowed for a moment, then the ground began to tremble, and the guards tried to slide to a stop as the earth split in front of them, but they couldn't stop in time. They both fell into the hole opening in the dirt, and hit the bottom of the pit with a loud *thud*.

Maurna looked in the hole she had made to see if the guards were still a threat and instantly cursed in her native tongue. One elf groaned as he fought to stay conscious, but the other began to howl out in pain as he looked at the large gash in his stomach from falling on his own sword. The mage continued to curse as orbs of light began to illuminate the kingdom.

The light came closer to the shadows that covered them, and she turned to Havish, Rust, and Saim to say, "Run!"

As they ran behind Maurna down the path, warning horns started blaring within the kingdom. It was clear that being stealthy was no longer a logical option. More horns sounded, but this time, they were closer.

Soon every man, woman, and child would be looking for the escaped prisoners, and the traitorous mage that released them. If they were caught, it was certain that death would immediately follow. That was, of course, if they weren't killed during the process of capture.

Soon the escapees found themselves at the kingdom's wall made from thick, tall trees fused together at their trunks. There was no way to reach a branch for climbing, and the tangled roots at the base made it impossible to even reach the tree itself. It was the end of the road, and the sound of many running footsteps of the Naughstaure guards were getting closer.

"To me!" Maurna called as she waved her hand.

They grouped together, readying their weapons for the oncoming onslaught, but the mage had a different idea. She raised her staff over her head, and as the jewel began to glow, the ground began to shake under their feet. Then they found themselves slowly lowering into the earth.

Soon, they were deep enough that all they could see was the night sky and the tree tops above, but their view was quickly obstructed by the dirt closing in over their heads. After a moment of moving in darkness the earth opened up again, and they were lifted to the surface, but on the other side of the wall of trees. Maurna had tunneled them to safety.

"Come," she ordered.

"Wait," uttered Rust. "I'm not going anywhere without Porter."

"He is safe," she sighed. "Now follow."

She darted into the dark woods away from the wall, followed by Havish and Saim, but the dwarf was a bit more reluctant to move. He looked back at the wall wondering if he could truly go on without his boar.

Before he could decide, he heard a squeal farther in the woods, and he cried out, "Porter?"

After a snort coming from the same direction, Rust ran as fast as his short legs would take him. He finally caught up to the half-elf and bard, and saw that they were mounting their horses. Nearby, his boar danced happily at the sight of his owner. The dwarf wasted no time, and rushed to Porter. He grabbed his mount's tusks and kissed him loudly on the snout.

"Thought you were staying behind, boy," Rust whispered.

Porter snorted, as if to scoff at the idea of leaving his owner's side, then nudged the dwarf to mount up. Rust obliged the boar's request and climbed upon his back.

Everyone looked to Maurna to lead the way, but she was preoccupied calling for her mount.

"Kymay!" she called.

Without warning, the trees began to quiver in the woods as something massive approached quickly. A growl could be heard coming closer, but the mage seemed unfazed by the oncoming sound. Everyone else glanced at each other nervously.

With a boom, a brown bear three times the size of a man burst through the tree line. It reared back on its back legs, as if to strike, and roared deep from its stomach. As it landed on its front paws, it glared at Maurna with its teeth bared. Saim pulled an arrow from his quiver, and pulled it back on his bow. Porter readied himself to pounce on the beast, as Havish and Rust tightened their grip on the handles of their weapons.

Maurna held out her hand to stop them from attacking, and mumbled something in elvish. As soon as she finished, the bear bowed down at her feet, and she quickly climbed on the beast's back. Saim lowered his aim and placed the arrow back in his quiver. The bard and the dwarf also put away their weapons, realizing this bear, Kymay, was no threat.

"They will follow us," the mage explained, "so we will have to ride all night to avoid recapture."

Just as Maurna turned to ride off into the woods, Saim asked, "Why are you helping us? I thought you wanted me executed."

"I do," she grumbled as she looked back at him. "You are an abomination. However, Faylin has other plans. And I don't dare question my king. Not even if it means disobeying the Elders."

Kymay quickly carried her off into the dark forest, and even though no one was completely sure they could trust this elf, they followed her into the unknown.

Chapter X

When Maurna was still a child, she spent a lot of her time sitting near the newly fallen leaves just outside the wall of Naughstaure. She loved when the seasons changed, because the tree tops would turn different shades of her favorite colors.

Elves were known for being attuned to nature, but many of the children in the kingdom thought she was daft for actually speaking to the plants. She would wish she could change colors like the leaves, and ask them in her native tongue how they did it.

"I don't mind if you speak to the leaves," Faylin said as he approached the child from the opening in the wall of the natural kingdom, "but could you practice speaking like the humans while you do it?"

She asked him why she should bother learning the language of the enemy, when she had never seen one, and doubted she ever would.

"They won't be our enemies forever," informed the king, "and if you do ever come in contact with one of their kind, you should be prepared."

"So they don't kill me like they did my parents?" Maurna finally said in the human language.

She always had a hatred for all things human, and Faylin wondered if it was the right thing to do by telling her the truth of how her mother and father met their end. It was a story of misunderstanding at a time after the war had ended, and Naughstaure was being created.

The new kingdom was in need of herbs for medicines for the sick and recovering soldiers, and when Maurna was only a short while from the womb, her parents ventured out to the woods near Cresience to collect them. They were found, caught, and not being able to explain themselves, they were executed for being sent to spy on the humans. Faylin blamed himself for getting them killed, so he vowed to take care of their child as his own.

"It's unfair that your parents died the way they did," the king mumbled as he sat on the ground next to the child. "But had they been able to communicate, things may have been different."

Though the king had gained his throne during the war between the races, he was still hopeful that peace would one day be restored. He believed being able to speak one another's language again was the first step. After all, the war was caused by a misunderstanding, and adding more blinders to the races' points of view wasn't going to make things better.

"Things may have been the same," Maurna groaned while waving her arm over the orange leaves. "I hate the humans."

The leaves, without the aid of touch or wind, scattered away from the child's hovering arm. With that, she stood and ran back into the kingdom. The king would have tried to follow her and calm her down but he was frozen in wonder.

Faylin wasn't sure what he had seen, and all he could do was whisper, "By the Great Spirit."

He was sure this was only possible if she were special. There was a reason she felt the need to speak to the trees, the plants, the bushes, and the dirt. She was connected to all of it. Not since the time of war was an elf selected by the Great Spirit for this purpose. She was a controller of nature. She was a mage.

...

The sun began to rise over the mountains in the distance as the travelers left the forest outside of Naughstaure. Maurna had never left the elven kingdom before, but somehow she just knew which direction to travel in order to reach Runehelm. This was one of the perks of someone with her ability.

Mages could never get lost, because the land always made them aware of their surroundings. Without proper training of her powers, she hadn't been made aware of this, but her instincts were strong. One thing she had always been brought up to do was follow those guiding voices from within her thoughts.

"How long before we reach our destination?" asked Havish.

"I think just couple of days travel," Maurna replied. "Maybe less."

"You think?" scoffed the bard.

Maurna pulled back on Kymay's loose skin on his neck to stop him, turned in frustration to Havish, and groaned, "Yes, I have a good idea of where we are headed, but if you think you know better, feel free to lead the way."

They glared at each other with distrust.

"If we're going where I think we're going, we're going the right way," Rust piped up.

"Where are we going?" questioned Saim.

"We're going to Runehelm," grunted the dwarf. "My home."

...

Food had become scarce in Runehelm. This was due in part to the dwarves' inability to mine for precious stones and metals any longer. Humans and elves believed that abysmyths had left once the Eye of Sight Unseen was placed in the dragons' nest in the Northern Continent. However, this was only because the dwarves had kept the remaining abysmyths at bay in the mines. Though the Door of Sight Unseen was shut, there was still the foul taint of these demons dwelling below the surface.

Unable to afford meat, the dwarves were forced to return to hunting for nourishment. The moment the red beard began to sprout from Rust's chin, he was forced to hunt with the other males. He loved the ability to prove himself to his people, so at the moment the sun rose he would arm himself and begin the hunt. This day he was especially excited, because there was a rumor of a mammoth boar in the meadows to the east. The meat from just one of its back legs would feed his entire tribe for days, and he was determined to catch it.

Rust had reached the tall grass of the meadow, crouched down to hide himself, and he closed his eyes to listen closely for the sound of any nearby beast. There was a rustling, but it was much too minute a sound to be his boar. He would not settle for anything less, so he stayed low to the ground, and continued to listen as he crawled through the tall blades of green. His fist tightly wrapped around his spear, and he made his way to the center of the meadow.

He knew if he waited long enough, he would catch a glimpse of the boar. So with his eyes closed to keep his ears open for any out-of-place noise, this was where he sat. Rust was ready for anything, and nothing would distract him. Except for maybe his gourde he filled with ale the night before.

Suddenly, Rust opened his eyes as something nudged his back. He found himself laying in the soft grass, and squinting in the sun. Realizing he must have fallen asleep in the warm glow of the morning, and the intoxicating contents of the now-empty gourde, he was completely unaware of the mammoth boar pushing to see if he was still alive.

The dwarf stayed still, planning a way to not only claim his kill, but not die in the process. The best idea he could come up with in the short amount of time was to roll to his feet, and scream triumphantly with his arms raised over his head.

The boar leapt back with a surprised squeal, and Rust immediately tossed his spear with all his might into the side of the boar. The tip stuck into the ribs of the boar, but was only deep enough to hang off of the beast's loose skin. This only angered the mammoth creature, and it responded by charging the dwarf at full speed.

Rust backed up nervously, but couldn't seem to find the right moment to turn and run. The boar lowered her large head, and rammed the dwarf with a force that threw him through the air high over the meadow. He landed on the ground with a thud, and groaned as all the air was forced from his lungs. Trying to shake the spots from his eyes, Rust looked up to see the beast running up to trample him.

The dwarf rolled out of the way, barely avoiding the massive and pounding hooves. As he lay in the tall grass trying to catch his breath, he watched the large boar run out of his sight with his spear. He cursed his lack of attention and his hunting ability as he pounded his fists on the ground.

Rust attempted to stand, but collapsed back onto the ground, shouting in pain. He looked down at his right thigh to see a deep gash from the tusk of his prey, and the blood had almost completely soaked his pants. It was clear that medical attention was needed, but his pride refused to let him give up. Even with a limp, he was still coming back with more meat than his tribe would ever be able to finish in one week. A feast was coming one way or another.

As the dwarf ripped his sleeve off of his shirt, he instantly noticed the wind picking up the cloth and making it wave to the south. A strong north wind moved through the grass in the meadow, and this was what gave Rust a new plan of action.

He tied the torn sleeve around his wound, and slowly got to his feet. Without the ability to run, he would need his prey to come to him. He would have to return to Runehelm for only a moment for a few supplies, but it wouldn't be long before he tasted sweet boar flesh.

After leaving his hut in the settlement, he brought with him a couple of flint rocks, a torch, his strongest drink in a canteen, and a hammer to put the gigantic beast down for good. Though Rust did drink half of the canteen to help him deal with the pain shooting through his thigh.

The dwarf went to the edge of the tall grass to the north, and poured the alcohol all over the top of the torch. With only two strikes of the flint rocks against each other, a spark lit the torch aflame. Then Rust poured the rest of the canteen along the edge of the meadow, saving the last sip for himself. He threw the torch in to the grass, and it instantly began to catch aflame.

Rust ran as quickly as he could go on only one good leg to the opposite end of the meadow. The wind carried the fire south, and the dwarf managed to get far ahead of it, where he waited for the retreating boar to come his way. Flames came closer, and Rust swung his hammer to practice his strike on the beast. The blaze was twice his height, so he knew the boar should be there at any moment. But the scorching fire reached the edge of the meadow, burning itself out.

The dwarf glared out into the smoldering grass, confused. Perhaps the mammoth boar found somewhere else to go, but how, without being seen? After a long while of staring out into the burnt field, he saw a large black mass in the distance. The foolish animal would rather burn alive than run for its life. Not putting up a fight for one's life seemed a ridiculous concept to Rust, which made him chuckle as he stepped onto the smoking earth.

Once he walked up to the large beast's charred corpse, his laughter faded. The beast lay on her side with her legs wrapped around four other smaller burnt bodies. She been trying to protect her children, but the fire had been much too large for her to shield. Rust had gotten his prey all right. He had claimed the whole family, and he had never felt more ashamed of himself.

A snort was heard from among the pile of burnt death. As the dwarf dropped to his knees, he reached into the corpse to pull free a baby boar. He was burned, but nothing that wouldn't heal in a few days. The pain of his wounds didn't seem to phase the young one. Maybe because his whole family had just been taken from the world, and his relatively new mind didn't know how to process this.

Something in Rust lit up with joy, and he couldn't explain it. Dwarves were not known for their maternal instincts, but as the little shoat squealed in his arms, Rust knew he could never cause harm to another of the piglet's kind. As the dwarf stood and carried the orphan out of what used to be a meadow, the guilt was replaced by a sense of purpose. This infant would grow up a happy and healthy boar. That was a promise.

...

Rust watched the campfire crackle as it spread across the wood they had collected earlier. The sun had set behind the mountains, the stars had come out to greet the moon, and the travelers had settled down for the night. Everyone was eating the salted meats from their packs, except for Maurna, who was eating a few fresh fruits and vegetables she had picked from the forest.

Silence had overtaken the group, which was odd considering Rust's presence. Saim looked at Havish and the mage, who'd had sour looks on their faces since they had left Naughstaure.

The bard felt like a failure from not being keep the half-elf safe, and Maurna felt livid because she had to. Having had enough of the tension, Saim decided to break the silence by turning to Rust.

"How long has it been since you have been in Rune-helm?" he asked the dwarf.

"Longer than I could keep track," replied Rust. "Longer than I care to remember."

The half-elf looked at the flame for a moment then said, "You don't seem to like the idea of going back."

"I don't, but you're paying me."

It was clear to Saim that conversation was not to be made easily, so he just looked to Porter, who was pushing some of his meal over to Kymay. The bear took the food gladly, after bumping her nose into the boar's cheek. Porter responded by snorting happily.

"Looks like your mount has made a new friend," chuckled the half-elf.

Rust looked up from the campfire and over to his boar. With a laugh, he said, "He's been that way since he was just a piglet. He's like dwarven mead. Strong, but too sweet for his own good."

Saim smirked, but realized he had never had a relationship as close as the dwarf and his boar. The longest amount of time the half-elf spent in one area was when he was in an orphanage. There, because of his deformed ears, he had been an outcast from the other children and potential parents. Before he could even attempt friendship with them, the children were either adopted or reached an age too old to stay.

Hardships outside the orphanage, Saim would find, were overwhelming. However, the young half-elf was ignorant to the ways of the world, and eventually ran away thinking there would be a place where he would be accepted. He was still looking for that place.

"You know," Rust interrupted the half-elf's thoughts. "Back in Naughstaure, Maurna said that horse saved your life. Guess that means she saved our lives too."

Saim nodded.

"Seems to me," continued the dwarf, "someone saves your life, you should, at the very least, know their name."

The half-elf glanced at Gormah's horse, who looked up from her oats to make eye contact with her new owner. She closed her eyes and bowed her head, as if to show respect to the person she carried. Then she went back to her oats.

"She doesn't have a name," Saim mumbled. "Besides, she's not my horse."

"You steal her?" asked Rust.

"No," the half-elf replied. "Her owner is dead."

"So you've been taking care of her since then?"

"Yes."

"Well," laughed the dwarf while taking the cap off of his canteen, "it sounds like she's your horse."

Rust took a quick drink of his ale, and held it out for Saim to take. The half-elf looked at the canteen for a moment, then decided to accept the dwarf's offer.

It was obviously a dwarven beverage, more concerned with its ability to inebriate than to be palatable. After choking down the abrasive drink, Saim coughed as he handed the canteen back.

"It takes some getting used to," Rust grumbled. "The flavor is off-putting at first, but if you stay true to it, it stays true to you."

The half-elf nodded with a smile, saying, "I must apologize for—"

"No," interrupted the dwarf, "I have done a lot of wrong in my time. It was only a matter of time before someone did what you did. Can't blame you for that."

"My thanks," Saim uttered.

Rust took another swig of his ale, and explained, "A dwarf never shares his drink. Accepting it when it happens is thanks enough."

The half-elf looked back at his horse, as Rust replaced the cap on his canteen and lay back on the large root behind him to get some sleep. Gormah's steed had finished snacking on the oats, and was settling down to get some rest as well. The dwarf was right. It was unfair to not name the being that had stuck with Saim since he began work at the farm, and had saved his life after bringing him all that way. One could say it was his oldest friend.

She needed a name, and only one could come to the half-elf's mind. The name of someone that he wished he had spent more time with when he was a child.

"Lurya," whispered the half-elf.

Rust, having almost drifted off from exhaustion, rolled over to ask, "Did you say something?"

"My horse," replied Saim, "her name is Lurya."

Chapter XI

"**I** know you are near, boy," boomed several voices in darkness, "and I'll find you."

Saim looked around, trying to find the source of the words, but only saw darkness and fog. He didn't know where he was, or how he had gotten there. In trying to get his bearings, he only knew that even though he couldn't see anyone, he wasn't alone. Continuous whispers echoed all around him, but were much too quiet to be understood.

"Where are you?" asked the half-elf. "Show yourself!"

"Stay where you are," the voices replied. "You will see soon enough."

The smell of sulfur soured the air, and a heat caused Saim to perspire. A red light shined from underneath him just as his feet began to blister. Pain shot through his body, and when he looked down to see what could be causing such discomfort, he saw that he was standing in molten lava.

He screamed as he sank into the bright, hot river. Around him, forms made of rock began to stand up from the lava. They had different heights and shapes, mimicking different beings, but their eyes were the same red illumination that flowed through their veins. These were the abysmyths.

The creatures surrounded Saim, and began to close in around him. Fear outweighed the agony of his dissolving legs, and he could only stare wide-eyed while the beasts of lava and rock came closer. It wasn't long before he was in arms' reach of the demons. Their long sharp fingers dug into his skin, and they began to pull his flesh from his bones. Fighting was useless, so he tilted his head back to shout away his last breaths.

...

Saim's eyes flew open, and he awoke in a cold sweat, gasping for breath. He looked to his fellow travelers, who were sleeping around the spent campfire. The morning was hidden in the trees behind them, and everything was still a blue hue. This would be an unreasonable hour to rise for most, but due to his past farm work, waking before sun had become a part of who he was.

The half-elf stood up, and stretched the stiffness out of his muscles. A few pops from his joints sent a relaxing shock through his spine. Careful not to wake anyone, he crept to his pack for his canteen. After a quick drink and a yawn, Saim splashed a little water on his face. Then he heard a screech echo through the sky.

He quickly wiped the water from his eyes and listened closely to ensure he truly heard it. Another shriek caused him to spin to the woods, though he knew whatever produced the sound was farther away than that. Nothing could be seen through the thick leaves, but he knew he had heard that noise before.

The half-elf quickly scaled a tree to get a view of the possible threat. Climbing was usually an easy task, but having been knocked around for the last few days, he was having a little trouble getting to the top branch. Once he found himself as high as he could go, the terror began to sink in, which kept him from catching his breath. All he could do was whimper.

Squinting into the rising sun, Saim could make out the silhouette of five dragons circling in the distance. Flame burst from their mouths, roaring, with a man on each of their backs. It wouldn't be long before the winged beasts were close enough to spot the travelers. Saim had to do something, and he couldn't take a lot of time doing it.

Attempting to quickly make his way down the branches was proving more difficult than going up. As soon as he put his weight on the last limb before the small drop to the ground, the wood gave way. Saim fell on his back, but he took only a moment to groan before he was back on his feet. He ran to Havish, who slept with a look of concern on his face, perhaps having a nightmare of his own. The half-elf thought it strange that there was once a time when he did everything in his power not to wake the bard, but there would be time to reflect on irony later.

"Havish," whispered Saim as he shook the sleeping human.

"What—?" groaned the bard just before the half-elf silenced him by clamping his hand over Havish's mouth.

Saim pointed to his mutilated ear to signal Havish to listen. It only took one screech from the distant dragons for the bard's eyes to widen with an understanding panic, so the half-elf took his hand away from his mouth. Havish immediately rolled to his feet and ran to Rust while Saim darted to Maurna. Both the elf and dwarf were shaken awake, and when they tried to talk, they were stifled with a hand.

The mage didn't take too kindly to being forced to consciousness in this fashion and shook her mouth away from the half-elf's hand, shouting, "Take your filthy hand off of me!"

Saim raised his finger to his lips, but she didn't seem to understand the expression of severity on his face.

"I will not be silenced!" she screamed. "What were you trying to do? Have your way with me?"

The bard shushed the elf and grumbled, "Would you stow your vanity and listen?"

Her brow furrowed with confusion until she heard the sound.

After her face melted into concern, and having never encountered the ominous noise, she whispered, "What is that?"

"Dragons," replied the half-elf with a terrified tremble in his voice.

"How many?" she asked, trying to keep her heart from stopping.

The screams of the flying monsters in the distance almost drowned out Saim's voice as he said, "A lot."

By this time, Havish and Rust had already gathered all their things and were climbing onto their mounts. Saim stood upright and held out his hand to help Maurna up, but she only stared at his palm.

"Would you just come on?" Rust begged impatiently while trying to catch a glimpse of the ambush.

It was still a bit before the airborne pirates would be close enough to see, which meant the travelers were still hidden as well. After finally taking hold of Saim's hand, the mage got up and quickly picked up her staff on the way to getting on Kymay's back. The half-elf ran to Lurya, who had already knelt down to allow him an easy way up.

Once Saim had mounted his horse, he felt the need to ask, "What do we do? If we run, they'll see us."

The dwarf only knew two ways of dealing with troubles, and seeing as how drinking wouldn't help them here, he suggested, "We stand our ground and fight."

"Don't be a fool," the bard scolded. "Judging by the sound alone, we're outmatched."

"Do you have a better idea?" asked Rust.

Havish, his confidence wrecked by the events in Naughstaure, searched his mind for any way out. He remained silent for only a few moments to formulate a plan, but it seemed like hours in the promise of imminent doom. His thoughts still drawing a blank, he groaned in frustration.

Maurna sighed and rode the bear in front of the travelers. She pointed her staff toward the treetops as the jewel on top began to glow. Suddenly, the woods groaned and creaked, then the leaves began to close in overhead, blocking the view of the sky.

"Stay close," she said as Kymay advanced into the woods. "Follow me."

The mage led them farther into the woods, and with every bit of ground they walked, the leaves closed out the light overhead. A dragon screamed as its large shadow floated across the ground nearby. Everyone froze, so not to make any noise, while breathlessly watching the winged black shape swoop by. Things seemed to worsen when another gigantic shadow was cast down next to the first.

Finally, the shadows moved on the ground behind the travelers, so they sighed with relief and continued forward. The sound of the sharp, scaly feet landing at their campsite rumbled through the trees. Not stopping for anything, the travelers continued to move stealthily, listening to the conversation of the pirates behind them.

"Still embers in the campfire," observed one of the buccaneers. "They've got to be close."

The other one scoffed, "They could have left it burning. They could already be in Runehelm."

"So we'll get them there."

"We even go near that place, their whole fleet will have our lives before you can soil your saddle."

"Well, they could still be close. Scout ahead, while the others search the forest."

With that, the dragons' wings flapped as the beasts took to the air. This would have been relieving to the travelers if a tree hadn't collapsed under another dragon's weight only a small walk away. Hoping Maurna knew where to take them, the travelers followed closely behind her, away from the grounded beast.

It wasn't long before they reached a cave, and the mage stopped outside. She waved everyone inside and then used the power of her staff to pull earth and rock to cover the cave entrance. Everything was dark, and everyone's stressful breaths echoed off of the hollow stone walls while they waited to see if they had successfully thwarted the searching eyes of their assailants.

"Did you hear that?" one of the pirates asked just outside the hidden cave entrance over the snarling of his dragon.

"Sounded like a rumbling," replied the other.

"Keep looking," commanded the first swashbuckler.

After the sound of the dragons' stomping quieted in the distance, Maurna whispered, "We may be here a while."

The jewel on her staff began to glow a bright white light, allowing everyone inside the cave to see clearly. She leapt off

Kymay's back, dug the bottom of the wooden rod into the dirt, and left it standing there as she walked to the stone wall to sit down.

Saim and Havish were trying to remain calm while they climbed off their horses. They were accustomed to open spaces, and having rarely been in confined quarters, panic began to set in. Rust, on the other hand, felt like he was back to working in the mines. Not even the stuffy air bothered him, but it was making it harder for the bard and half-elf to breathe.

Every sound made Saim and Havish look around nervously, but it was only typical underground noises: dripping moisture, rocks tumbling from farther within, and their own echoes. Rust and Maurna would smirk at each other over the rest of the group's unease, until something that sounded like whispers traveled from the cavern.

"Did someone say something?" asked the mage.

Everyone shook, their heads with eyes widened, as they looked into the black unknown. Their heartbeats were all they could hear as they waited for another noise to come from the cave, but the only thing they noticed was a slight rise in the temperature and the smell of something burning. Porter and Kymay both began to growl while the horses stepped around nervously. Something was coming.

Finally, thin lines glowing orange, red, and yellow could be seen in the darkness. They almost looked like lava flowing through cracks in the wall, but they looked as if they were coming closer. It became clear that they were illuminated veins for some being. Eyes reflected crimson in the glow of the mage's staff, and a growl escaped from the unknown beast's mouth.

As it walked into the magic light, the details of the creature could be seen. It was made of ash and rock, and lava flowed through its veins. The sharp claws made of what looked like black shiny glass dragged the dirt of the cave. When its mouth opened to roar, an unintelligible barrage of whispers could be heard.

True to his dwarven roots, it was Rust who could identify the demon.

"Abysmyth."

Chapter XII

Long before Rust left his home, he swung his pickaxe with all his youthful might, piercing the stones inside a deep mine near Runehelm, desperately attempting to bring profit back through his colony. With his boar by his side, and all day long for a week, he worked to exhaustion with nothing yet to show for it. But he was not going to give up, until he found a fortune of jewels and metal ore.

The mines had been closed since before Rust was born. The rumor was five dwarves had lost their lives to an abysmyth attack. Most dwarves were to too afraid to walk into the caves in case it was true, but Rust knew if he didn't get wealth back into his home, it would mean he would have to part with things that were priceless in his eyes.

Porter had grown to a full-sized mammoth boar, and he would help his owner by moving the loose rocks out of the way. It wasn't much help, but if anything, the dwarf was happy to have the company. And they were inseparable. They ate together, they washed in the river together, and they even shared a bed for sleep. Well, it was more like Porter let Rust have a small fraction of the bed. It was the strangest friendship to all the dwarves in Runehelm.

The dwarf struck the rock once more to knock a large chunk of stone free. After picking up the piece of rock, he carried it to his lantern sitting on a nearby dirt mound. Tilting the stone from side to side, he inspected it carefully, looking for any reflection of light. There was none.

He sighed and threw the rook over his shoulder saying, "Maybe we should take a break."

The boar groaned in agreement, and rested next to the dirt mound Rust was sitting on. The dwarf pulled some meat out of his pack to eat, but stopped when he heard a growl.

"Okay," he grumbled as he tore off a piece for his boar. "Don't be so impatient."

However, as Rust tried to feed the meat to Porter, he noticed the boar was looking elsewhere. On the far end of the mine, a small, glowing, orange dot could be seen. The dwarf perked up, thinking it was the glint of something valuable, but his excitement quickly changed to fear as the dot grew bigger. It was lava, and it was melting through the wall.

Waves of heat filled the cavern while Porter and Rust prepared to rush out of the mine, but it was too late. The rim of the new hole shimmered with molten rock, and that's when It walked through. Dwarven tales spoke of this creature with such detail, that the young dwarf knew exactly what it was. It was an abysmyth, and it was looking right at them.

After a long ear-piercing scream, it charged Rust, lifting its clawed hand out for a swipe. Just before it could swing its arm, Porter rammed his tusks into its side, tossing it into a wooden support beam. The plank instantly snapped in half, and caught aflame. Rock and dirt fell onto the abysmyth from above, pinning it for a moment.

Rust looked over at Porter, who was snorting in pain from the small burns on his snout. The dwarf owed the boar his life in more ways than one, so he pushed Porter past the trapped creature to the mine's entrance tunnel. The monster swung its claws, just barely missing them. Never taking his eyes off of the infuriated abysmyth, the dwarf pressed his back against the wall, and slowly followed his boar. However, when the creature wrapped its large clawed hand around one of the stones and moved it to the side, Rust decided to take the opportunity to turn and run.

Agony shot through the dwarf's back as the abysmyth reached out to Rust. Its claws swiped across his back, slicing him deep. As it held onto his burlap shirt, the dwarf howled in pain and fear for his life. This got his boar's attention.

Porter turned around, ran to the support beam near Rust, and kicked it, breaking it in two. A boulder fell out of the ceiling of the mine, and landed on the abysmyth's head. Lava began to flow out from the creature's lifeless body, and slowly run toward other planks in the cavern. Once the molten rock touched the wood, it caught fire. The dwarf's eyes widened as he realized what this would mean. Cave in.

As soon as Rust climbed on his boar's back, the support beams gave under the pressure of the stone and earth. Porter quickly carried them out of the mine shaft that was collapsing behind them. The falling planks, rock, and dirt were coming closer in what seemed to be a never-ending cave. Finally light could be seen at the end of the tunnel, so the boar gave every last bit of speed he had left.

They flew out of the entrance to the mine, followed by a cloud of dust. After taking a moment to let the fact that they survived soak in, Rust sighed with relief. He never thought he would see an abysmyth in person, let alone have to battle with one. But this proved two things to the dwarf: the legendary beast was real, and more importantly, it could be killed. It was one of the many lessons he would never forget.

...

Rust sneered at the abysmyth walking closer to the travelers, and shouted, "Maurna, prepare to bury him! Everyone else, stay back!"

With that, the dwarf charged at the beast while he pulled his massive hammer from his back. After a few steps he was close enough to duck under the swiping arm of the monster, then Rust brought his weapon back for a mighty blow. The abysmyth stumbled back as the war-hammer met the side of its face, causing a burst of sparks to fall on the dwarf's shoulders. Then with another hard strike of his steel, he took out the creature's legs from under him.

"Now!" commanded Rust.

Saim grabbed the staff from the dirt, and tossed it to Maurna. She caught it, instantly pointing the jewel toward the ceiling above the beast. As it began to stand on its broken appendages, the cave collapsed, and completely hid its body under the rocks.

After a moment passed to catch their breath, Havish said, "We will run out of air much sooner now."

"There was no other way," explained Rust.

"I know," agreed the bard.

"Half-elf," the mage uttered with a look on her face that seemed like gratitude. "Don't ever touch my staff again."

Saim sighed in frustration, but this was interrupted by the movement of the stones piled on the abysmyth. Rust glared at the rubble as an orange glow began to seep through the cracks between the rocks.

"We're not done yet," announced the dwarf. "We have to flee!"

"What if the dragons are still out there?" asked Maurna.

"The threat is greater in here!" Rust exclaimed.

"He's right," Havish agreed. "Mount up. We're leaving."

Everyone climbed upon their rides just as the trapped creature freed its arm. The abysmyth used its clawed hand to dig itself out from under the rocks, while the travelers waited for the mage to open the cave in front of them.

Holding her staff overhead, moving the earth in front of the cave entrance, she shouted, "Be ready to run with everything you've got!"

The rocks fell away from the opening, which pulled fresh and cool air into the cavern. Once the wind hit their faces they all rode their mounts out of the cave as quickly as the animals could carry them. With no enemy in sight, they ducked under branches and leaves, making their way to freedom.

Suddenly, a dragon landed hard in front of them, digging its claws into the ground to stop itself. Both the flying mount and the pirate on its back looked directly at the travelers, who just turned to go around the dragon. Before the swashbuckler could attempt to attack or follow them, he saw the abysmyth that had escaped from the cave, and the fire the creature left behind with every step.

The pirate screamed but was quickly silenced by the monster knocking his dragon on its side. As the abysmyth leapt on top of the dragon's fallen body, it grabbed its scaly neck and pulled it off of its body.

Horrified, the buccaneer turned to run from the monster and his mount's deceased, bloody corpse. But before he could get too far, the abysmyth backhanded the pirate, sending him flying through the air and into a thick tree.

The man may have died with the impact of the monster's hand, or he could have died when he slammed against the bark. Regardless, his body was broken, blood-soaked, and lifeless.

Still running, the travelers were gaining distance from the abysmyth, but the creature wanted their blood, and followed. Another dragon began to circle overhead, unaware of the horror still in the woods. It swooped down for an attack on the mage just as the bloodthirsty monster tore a tree from the ground, and threw it at the dragon.

Struck by the uprooted oak, the winged mount fell a great distance to the ground, crushing the pirate underneath him. The dragon roared, trying to get back on its feet, but it was clear that it had broken one of its legs. The abysmyth rushed toward the fallen dragon, whose only defense was spewing fire onto its already blistering rock flesh. The beasts swung their clawed hands, trying everything to end the other's life.

This was the perfect distraction for the travelers to escape. The battle behind them shrunk in the distance, and it finally seemed that they were going to get away. That was until they heard the cry of another dragon above them. Before they could look up, it swept down, and grabbed Maurna off of Kymay's back with its clawed feet.

It flapped its wings to carry her and the pirate on its back away, but before it could get far, an arrow flew through the air, striking its leg. The mage fell with a thud, and tumbled on the ground for a bit. She turned to the direction of the fired projectile only to see Saim pulling another arrow from his quiver.

The dragon turned to launch a deadly breath at the half-elf, but at the moment it began to exhale, the arrow flew from the bow, piercing the roof of its mouth.

It fell lifeless to the ground beside Maurna, and the pirate riding it had his leg pinned under its massive weight. Saim, shocked by his weapon's accuracy, rode up to her, climbed off Lurya's back, and helped the elf to her feet. She was speechless as she looked into his eyes. She had met his gaze before, but this was the first time she really looked deeper.

"Saim," she whispered.

The half-elf jerked his hand away from hers, worried that she was about to scold him, "Sorry."

"Saim," she called, meeting his eyes again. "Thank you."

Finally, they shared a moment other than disdain, and the half-elf couldn't help but smile. This was different from Rust, who climbed off of Porter with a murderous scowl on his face, and marched over to the trapped buccaneer.

The dwarf lifted his hammer for a killing blow, but Havish shouted, "No!"

Rust looked back at the bard with a look of confusion, asking, "Why?"

"We can question him," Havish explained. "Find out what he knows of Separ's plan."

Everyone agreed this was the best possible plan, but it didn't mean the dwarf wasn't disappointed that he couldn't take out his aggression on the pirate. He hoped he could be the one to beat the truth out of him later.

"Get some rope," commanded the bard as he turned to Saim and Maurna.

He was going to say more, but he could only gasp when he saw the hulking abysmyth reappear over the hill behind them. Dragon blood sizzled on the surface of its flesh, and lava poured from new cracks in its body. It was hurt, but it was also angry.

Everyone backed up, knowing there was no escape this time as the abysmyth charged toward them. Saim quickly fired an arrow, but it just bounced off of the creature's stone flesh. The travelers were certain it would be futile to fight, but they all grouped together to defend themselves.

Just as the abysmyth raised its clawed hand over its head to make its first kill, something *whoosh*ed across the sky and impaled the monster's chest. It stumbled backward, screaming, trying to pull out a large bolt from a ballista. Life was quickly draining from the abysmyth's body as it fell to the ground.

"Finish it off!" commanded a deep, gravely voice behind the travelers. "Any living pirates are coming with us."

They turned to see a small army of dwarves advancing from behind with four large bulls towing a towering ballista on wheels. Large swords, axes, and hammers in hand, the dwarves ran past the travelers to the dying monster. As they easily pummeled the remaining life from the creature, one dwarf approached the travelers while sheathing his sword on his back.

"You hurt?" he asked.

They replied by shaking their head.

"Good," he said as he held out his stubby hand to greet the travelers. "We are only a short travel away from town, so let me be the first to welcome you to Runehelm."

Chapter XIII

Runehelm was like nothing Saim had ever seen before. Its buildings were small stone structures and not very significant, but the machinery that was once used for mining the mountain nearby had been reworked to provide transport, heat, and water for the city. The noise of escaping steam, turning gears, and flowing liquid drowned out any gasps of awe from and half-elf.

Rust, however, dreaded being back in this place. To the dwarves living here, he was an outcast, a traitor to his people and what they stood for.

As the travelers continued past the bull stables at the edge of town, the dwarven general turned to the travelers and said, "We're going to drop the pirate off at the jail and return to patrol, but feel free to spend a little coin. We have an inn, a tavern, a smith, and plenty of shops. Everything you could want or need."

After some thanks from the travelers, he nodded, and led his army back into the wild. A couple of soldiers split from the group to take away the limping buccaneer, who held his side, groaning with every step.

The once mining colony was scattered with only a few dwarves, mostly women and children. The only males that could be seen were tilling the soil at the nearby farm, cutting wood, or working on the machinery in the center of the town.

A few others fished on the pier, where large ships were docked with sails towering far above them. Blocky, metal depictions of animals jutted out from the fronts of the ships, providing sturdy and beautifully crafted rams. Ballistas peered through the windows along the sides of the vessels, and larger ones sat on the decks. They were exceedingly finer warships than any human hand could create.

As everyone gawked in wonder at the massive boats, one of the dwarven men working on the elaborate water pump turned to the travelers atop their mounts.

"Welcome to Runehelm," he greeted as he walked over, extending a dirty hand. "Name's Kragg."

The dwarf's smile faded slowly into a scowl when Rust turned to meet his eyes.

"Hello, brother." Rust said. "It's been a while."

...

Before Rust had ever left his home town, he sat at the dinner table with his younger sibling, Kragg. They teased each other over love interests in the village as their mother, Ruby, placed their meal on the table. Once she sat down, everyone looked at the skimpy meal of bread and fish stew that was mostly broth. When her boys exchanged a look with disappointment in their eyes, Ruby's welled up with tears.

It was a struggle to provide for her family ever since their father, her husband, died in a cave-in just before the mines closed. The good people of Runehelm helped all they could by offering them food from their households, but trade and profit was low since the colony could no longer produce precious stones and ore. The whole town had trouble feeding themselves, which meant the needy were even worse off.

Rust and Kragg looked to Ruby trying to hide her tears, and instantly forced smiles on their faces. They quickly broke the bread into three small but equal parts, and filled their bowls with the stew.

"Looks great," complimented Rust.

"This is exactly what I was in the mood for," agreed Kragg.

Ruby quickly wiped her tears away and lovingly stared at her children, saying, "You don't have to do that."

The young dwarven boys looked up from their bowls, innocently asking, "Don't have to do what?"

She shook her head, and they all continued to eat what little nourishment they had in front of them. The home didn't have a lot of money or food, but had more love than any in Runehelm.

After dinner, Rust went to his room with some scraps he didn't eat. He did this every meal since he brought Porter home with him. Often, he would go to bed hungry to make sure his boar stayed happy and healthy. The affection of his beast was enough to sustain him for months. But the dwarf wasn't aware that Porter would too starve himself so that his owner wouldn't die of hunger. It wasn't a good situation for either of them, but it was the one they had, and they were making the best of it.

As the boar began to eat the scraps, Kragg entered the bedroom. Rust turned to see the look of concern on his brother's face.

"I've got to speak to you," Kragg announced, waving his hand signaling to come along with him.

Rust stood and followed his brother out of his bedroom, through the living area, and out the door leading outside. He waited for Kragg to speak, but he only looked around with his mouth teasing the beginning of a sentence.

"Well?" Rust asked. "What is it?"

With a sadness in his eyes, his brother said, "Since father's passing, things have been difficult for us."

"Aye," agreed the redheaded dwarf.

"Mother has been struggling. She's hungry, and she knows we are as well. I tire of watching her become upset, and I tire of being hungry."

"As do I."

"I'm glad you agree. Perhaps this request will not be as shocking."

"What are you getting at?"

"Mother and I have been talking and we both agree," Kragg sighed. "He's gotten quite large. Wouldn't you say?"

"Who?" questioned Rust. "Porter?"

Kragg nodded to his brother, who scowled, knowing what he was trying to hint. To that Rust said, "You had better not be implying what I think you are."

"We don't have a choice," explained Kragg. "With all that meat—"

"That *meat* is Porter," Rust interrupted.

"We could eat for a month. He's lived a good life."

"He's one of us! We don't eat our own!"

"He's a boar! We are dwarves! He is not one of us!"

"Then neither am I," Rust groaned as he turned to the door of his home.

"He's just another mouth to feed, brother. We can't afford that, and we can't afford for you to not give him up."

Rust stopped, and turned to Kragg. He was right. Ruby, Rust, and his brother fought to only scrape by. Love was thick in this home, but was it enough to keep suffering?

Kragg pulled a dagger from his belt, and whispered solemnly, "I can do it for you. You won't have to see it. He won't feel a thing."

"No," Rust uttered, taking the blade from his brother. "I should do it. It has to be me."

"Are you sure?"

With tears in his eyes, the redheaded dwarf nodded to Kragg and walked back inside his home. The journey from the front door to his room was lengthier than anything he had done before. Every step was hesitant to start and end. His hands shook around the handle of the dagger. Everything in his body told him to stop, but yet he pushed forward.

As Rust opened his bedroom door, Porter greeted him with a snort. The dwarf hid the blade, and he approached with a heavy heart. Sensing that something was wrong, the boar came closer and nuzzled Rust's side. He sobbed and wrapped his arms around Porter's neck.

"I'm sorry," he whimpered, and he placed the dagger under the boar's chin.

Unable to go through with the slaughter, he threw the blade to the ground. If they couldn't afford to have Porter, he would make it even easier on them. His mother and brother would be better off, with food to spare between one another. But that food would never be his boar. Porter was leaving, and Rust was going with him.

...

It seemed like so long ago the young dwarf and his boar had gone missing that one night. Kragg couldn't believe his eyes, but there was no questioning this was his brother, and the beast he was crawling off of was Porter. As Rust walked closer, a scowl came over Kragg's face. And before the redheaded dwarf could get a word out of his mouth, his brother struck him with a balled-up fist.

As Rust recovered from the blow, Havish thought aloud, "Is this how everyone deals with him?"

Rust charged at Kragg, and they instantly resorted to unarmed combat. The travelers leapt off their mounts and ran to break up the fight. At that moment, a Runehelm jailor came out of the dungeon to separate the two.

Havish and Saim pulled their sword-for-hire away from his brother, who too was being restrained.

"You shouldn't have come back!" shouted Kragg.

"You shouldn't have hit me!" replied Rust.

"You shouldn't have left!"

"You gave me no choice!"

"You broke Mother's heart!"

"She has you!"

"She's dead!"

Rust was speechless. The half-elf and bard felt the fight go out of his body, so they released his arms.

"Mother?" the dwarf's voice shook. "She's dead?"

Kragg pulled himself free from the Runehelm jailor and said, "Aye."

As silence overcame the town, the jailor walked up to Havish, informing him that, "The pirate is ready for your questions."

Everyone looked to Rust to see what he wanted to do. Had the situation been different, the bard would have just demanded they all go. But having just received the news of his mother's demise, no one felt it right to make decisions for him.

"You go ahead," Rust grumbled to the travelers. "My brother and I have some things to discuss."

With that, Havish nodded and turned to lead Maurna and Saim to the dungeon. The jailor took their mounts to the stables, leaving Kragg and Rust alone.

After a moment of glaring at one another in a contemplative silence, the redheaded dwarf asked, "Where is she?"

"Come," replied his brother. "I'll take you to her."

As Rust followed Kragg to the Warrior Temple, the rest of the travelers entered the door of the dungeon.

Inside the dungeon, a dwarven guard stood next to the cell holding the buccaneer they had captured. With their arrival, the guard pulled out a key and unlocked the cell door. Silently, he pushed the door open and waved the remaining travelers inside. Havish, Maurna, and Saim walked inside the cell, the door shutting behind them.

The pirate sat on a cot attached to the stone wall by thick chains, and he rubbed the leg that had been trapped under his dead dragon. He seemed too busy wincing in pain to notice he was no longer alone in his cell.

Havish still felt angry from the ambush earlier, and seeing this swashbuckler again only reignited that fury. The bard quickly closed the distance between them, grabbed the pirate's throat, and put his knee into his injured thigh.

Howling in pain, the buccaneer silenced himself as Havish asked, "How are you tracking us?"

"I won't betray Separ for you," hissed the swashbuckler. "And he will have the half-elf's life."

The bard dealt the pirate a blow across the face with the back of his hand, then said, "Your kind have stolen more ships than the people of Runehelm can keep up with. I assure you these dwarves will show no mercy in your punishment. I, however, can make things easy on you."

"You can't promise such things."

"Perhaps you shouldn't doubt the only man offering you compassion. Separ is a tyrant, so I understand your reluctance to speak. But I know he has told your men to stay clear of Runehelm. He knows this army would take more lives than he could afford to lose. You will be safe from the Dragon's Voice, but only if you tell me what I want to know."

The pirate's eyes squinted as if he were putting serious consideration into Havish's words, but after a few moments, he spit in the bard's face. Havish pulled the buccaneer to the ground, and brought him to one of the chains at the edge of the cot.

"Hold his arms," the bard ordered.

Maurna and Saim held the swashbuckler's arms while Havish lifted the cot to put slack in the chain. After wrapping the loose links around the pirate's neck, the bard pushed on the cot, causing the chain to tighten around the buccaneer's neck. Sweat began to collect on the swashbuckler's brow.

"You feel that?" asked Havish. "What do you think will happen if I were to have a rest? Now, tell me how you've been tracking us."

The pirate said nothing, so the bard began to put his weight on the cot. As the eyes bulged out of the buccaneer's face, the veins in his forehead began to show through his tightening skin. Finally, a gurgle escaped the swashbuckler's throat, so Havish took his hand away from the cot.

"We've been tracking you since Cresience!" coughed the pirate. "For as long as I can remember, we've been looking for the half-elf. But it wasn't until Cresience that someone knew of him. Some barkeep."

"How did you find us this time?" interrogated the bard.

"Separ knew you would be headed to Naughstaure!" the buccaneer exclaimed. "It was there we found out you were on the way to Runehelm."

"You went to Naughstaure?" asked Maurna with panic in her eyes.

"Yes," replied the pirate.

"Did you hurt anyone?"

"No, I scouted ahead, but the rest—" The swashbuckler stopped, looking at his interrogators with dread.

"By the Great Spirit!" Maurna yelled. "What did your people do?"

"They—" The buccaneer's words stumbled out of his mouth. "They burned it to the ground."

Tears welled in the elf's eyes. Her home, everyone she loved, everything she ever knew and loved was gone. In only a moment she had lost more than just the man who raised her. She had lost it all. All of it.

She let go of the pirate's arm and walked to the front of the cot. Saim and Havish watched the expression on her face, but could not read it. After she wiped a tear from her eye, with no warning, she dropped down with all her weight. The sounds of the chain going taut and his collapsing windpipe were the last noises the swashbuckler would ever hear.

...

The Warrior Temple was where the people of Runehelm put their dead to rest. Brass and golden statues of legendary dwarves, both warriors and inventors, lined the marble walls. Torches hung on stone pillars, and their light danced on the metallic decorations framing the corners of the structure and causing the many headstones of lost dwarven ancestors to glisten.

There, in one of the frequent halls of the temple, Rust and Kragg stood by the marked stone for their mother Ruby. Both were silent as they looked at her stone encasement.

"How did it happen?" asked the redheaded dwarf.

"You left. She got sick. She died. That's how."

The brothers glared at each other with disdain. It was clear that Kragg blamed her death on Rust, but his reason for leaving was justified in his mind.

"You can't blame me for leaving," the redheaded dwarf groaned. "You both wanted to kill my boar."

"No," Kragg began, "I did. Only me."

Rust furrowed his brow in confusion and betrayal. All this time, he thought his mother and sibling had chosen the fate of Porter.

"You deceived me," Rust said through gritted teeth. "I trusted you."

"She would never agree to it, but I knew it was in our best interest."

"You made me miss out on my mother's last days!" Rust shouted as he grabbed the collar of Kragg's dirty, burlap shirt, and he slammed his sibling into the marble wall. "Damn you!"

"I didn't make you leave! It was the ridiculous attachment you have to that mammoth boar! You abandoned your family for an animal."

"I left so no one would have to die, and there would be less mouths to feed."

"We didn't want you gone!" Kragg shouted, pushing his brother away. "I wanted my brother here! Mother wanted you here!"

"And you drove me away from her!"

"I was trying to save our family!"

Rust took a deep breath to keep himself from striking his sibling, and after moving his crimson hair out of his face, he grumbled, "Did she go peacefully?"

"She asked for you, but I didn't know how to find you," explained Kragg as he leaned against his mother's stone casket. "I didn't know you were traveling with adventurers. What even brings you this way?"

"I'm guarding them. Came here to acquire a ship."

"I see," said Kragg as he got to his feet. "But I think you should know something."

He walked closer to Rust, and took a deep breath, before continuing.

"Not long after Mother's death, the people of this settlement elected someone to lead them. Someone who gave them hope of a future where no man, woman, or child would have to sacrifice as much as we did just to fight off hunger. They elected me."

Rust didn't know where his brother was going with this, but he humored him by mumbling, "Congratulations."

"Let me finish," Kragg uttered. "When they elected me, I brought Runehelm back from poverty by making the best ships for any need. We've done well. And every boat we sell ensures the health of my people for a long time. That being said, I want you aware of the sacrifice I am making for this spitefulness."

"What are you—?"

"I'm saying," interrupted Kragg, "I mean no offense to your friends, but they have chosen the wrong dwarf for their mission. You will never have one of my ships. Never."

After that, Rust's brother left the temple, leaving the redheaded dwarf and the insult stewing. It was at this very moment that the sellsword decided a new plan of action.

Before leaving, Rust placed his hand on the stone grave and whispered to his lost mother, "I'm sorry."

...

The sun had fallen behind the ocean, and the travelers were resting at the inn. Rust was not with them, but had let them know he was going to be getting them a ship if it was the last thing he would do. Since he and his brother had quite a disagreement, and the jailors were furious at the death of their prisoner, this would not be an easy task.

One would think from the nights spent on the cold dirt of campsites, that Havish, Saim, and Maurna would be able to easily fall asleep. However they were all troubled by the events of the day. They were all taken aback by the appearance of an abysmyth, but bard and half-elf were more concerned about the unknown road ahead.

Maurna hadn't said a word since killing the prisoner. Noticing her plight, Saim looked to the mage and tried to comfort her with an apology. She looked to him with tears in her eyes but said nothing before returning her gaze to the wooden floorboards.

"I know nothing I could do would help," he continued, "but if there's anything—"

"You're right," she interrupted. "Nothing you could do will help. Nothing but not coming to Naughstaure in the first place."

Saim could only nod in agreement. It seemed anywhere he went, trouble followed. It had started with his mother and hadn't stopped since. Everyone sacrificed so much for him, and he wasn't positive he was worth it.

"Saim did not slay your people," Havish uttered. "Nor did Rust. Nor did I. It was Separ. He is your enemy. Saim, however, is the only one of us who could even relate to your despair."

Maurna looked at the bard with a scowl.

"You're upset," continued Havish. "You have every reason to be. But know your enemy. You will have your revenge. And we will assist you in doing so."

The hatred left the elven mage's face as she realized the truth in his words, and she nodded in gratitude. They had a common opponent, and her king knew of the danger. That's why he sent her with them. That's why he sacrificed himself.

Just as everyone prepared to rest for the night, Rust burst through the door with a look of determination, saying, "Gather your things."

The travelers turned to him, not yet understanding the desperation in his eyes.

"I've got us a ship," the dwarf informed them, "but we have to leave. Now!"

Chapter XIV

"**I**f only we had thought of making these during the war," said the salesman. "But, alas, we hadn't yet closed the mines. Luckily, the Kingdom Alliance still uses them to police the seas against pirates."

Rust glared at the hulking ships in the orange setting sun as he walked along the creaking wooden pier with the dwarf responsible for every vessel at the docks of Runehelm. Neglecting to mention the elected ruler of the settlement had refused any business to him, the redheaded dwarf asked detailed questions about every boat they passed. Questions about speed, durability, strength of the hull, weaponry, and size of the crew needed for operation. It was becoming more apparent the only ship the travelers could use would be much smaller than the massive warships used by armies.

The advantage of these smaller ships was that they could be manned by only a few crewmen, the sails could carry the weight of the vessel more quickly, and they could steer through crevasses the larger warships couldn't dream of. Even though the disadvantages weren't as numerous, the severity of the disfavor outweighed them easily. Less weaponry, and it wouldn't take much to sink it.

A dwarf knew nothing about defensive strategies, so knowing it would be necessary for flight rather than fight seemed a foreign concept. But nonetheless, a concept Rust would have to grow accustomed. The crew would be too small for a warship, but for what they would lack in size, they would make up for in will.

"So," the salesman interrupted the redheaded dwarf's thoughts, "which ship catches your eye?"

"Oh, I'm sorry to mislead," laughed Rust. "Your leader, Kragg, has denied me purchase of one of your fine vessels. 'Twas only curious, and you've been very helpful. My thanks."

He patted the ship salesman on the shoulder, and walked away. Having spent hours explaining each boat and how to sail them, the salesman watched with his mouth agape in disbelief as the red-bearded dwarf left.

...

Rust peered out of the crack of the slightly ajar wooden door, and after seeing the empty hall, he pulled the door open. A quick motion of his hand told the rest of the travelers to follow as he stepped into the hall.

Soon they all found themselves down the stairs and in the tavern of the inn, where only a few drunken dwarves remained. A bar keep was also among the sparse patrons, but he was a little too busy wiping clean tankards to pay any mind to the town's visitors.

In only moments, the travelers were outside the inn and in the empty, dark settlement. All was quiet but the chirping insects, the various machinery, and the splashing waves at the shore. Keeping an eye on the surroundings, Rust continued to crouch along the ground, making his way to the stables, followed by his companions.

The stables were quiet, except for the occasional snort of one of the bulls or their mounts. Apparently, Runehelm never had an issue of someone stealing from them in a while, because no guard was stationed outside. However, things were made more difficult when the travelers noticed a large gauge chain and lock around the stable doors.

"Damn," hissed Rust.

"What happened with your brother?" asked Havish.

"Now's not the time to discuss such things," the dwarf replied. "Help me get this lock off."

"It would seem to be the perfect time," said the bard as he moved between Rust and the door. "Since it's clear we are sneaking around."

The dwarf looked everyone in the eyes, and finally decided to come clean. "He's denied us a ship, so we're taking one."

The travelers were speechless, until Maurna sighed, "So be it."

She touched the jewel on her staff to the lock, which instantly began to glow red. The links of the chains went slack as the lock melted off of the door. As the glowing metal cooled upon the ground, Rust pulled open the door and peeked inside.

Before he could get a view of the stable, a wet snout appeared in front of his face. Porter must have sensed the dwarf's anxiousness, because he was waiting at the door with Havish's horse, Kymay, and Lurya. Quickly the travelers led their mounts out of stable and out into the open.

Rust crept to the pier with everyone close behind, each one with their animals in tow. It seemed the whole town was asleep, because not one dwarf, other than the sellsword they had guiding them, could be seen.

Their movement was silent, but as they stepped foot on the wooden docks, the sound of their steps became harder to muffle. The hooves of the horses and the boar knocking on the boards made it clear that stealth was no longer an option. Now it was a task of haste.

With the passing of every large ship, Saim, Maurna, and Havish felt the anticipation of wondering to which large vessel they were going. The massive size of the boats they were passing could only mean they were getting on one that was even bigger. However, when they stopped at the ship Rust had selected, disappointment washed over them. With only one sail, one ballista, a simple stable, and the smallest of living quarters, it was the most minuscule vessel at the pier.

"You can't be serious," whispered the bard in disbelief.

The dwarf turned to Havish with a scowl and informed him, "We don't have a crew. What did you expect?"

Suddenly, the sounds of alarm bells could be heard from within Runehelm. Rust's jaw dropped as he noticed an on-coming army of dwarves. The bard looked back, and without a word led his horse up the ramp leading to the deck. Rust and Saim followed with Porter and Lurya, but stopped when they noticed that Maurna was not behind them. The elf looked into Kymay's eyes, and said something in elvish.

"What are you doing?" asked Saim in a panic.

"She's saying goodbye," replied Havish as he waved the half-elf and the redheaded dwarf to hurry onto the vessel.

The bear pressed his snout against Maurna's face, knowing this may be the last time the mage would ever be seen. After one last look into each other's eyes, Kymay left the elf's side, running toward the onslaught of dwarves.

The army quickly moved out of the way, swinging their weapons futilely, not striking the bear. Kymay continued through Runehelm, and back into the wilderness. Although not taking a single dwarven life, the bear still provided enough time for Maurna to run aboard the small ship.

"Why did you send him away?" asked Saim.

"Though I have no home to go back to," she explained, "Kymay still does."

The bard, half-elf, and mage placed their animals in the stables as Rust cut the ropes connecting the ship to the docks, calling out the orders, "Havish, man the wheel! Saim, take the ballista! Maurna, help him with the bolts! I'll deal with the sails!"

"Do you even know what you're doing?" asked the bard.

The dwarven sellsword turned to Havish and shouted, "We're about to find out!"

...

It was not long after Rust began to sell his services as a guard that he was hired by a wealthy employer, who needed his treasured family heirlooms delivered to his new home to the north. The dwarf knew moving the priceless cargo by land would be too risky with the many bandits that camped out along the trails, so he asked that his employer get a ship to carry it to a nearby port. Then from the port, he could move the treasure by wagon to the location. It was a good plan, but even the best plans could find trouble along the way.

Of course, a wealthy client would do all he could to save his mountains of gold, so he hired a crew that could only be described as morally questionable. Rust didn't trust the sailors, but he could only keep a heedful eye on the men. His opinion of the crew, he would find, was not just paranoia.

The dwarf spent most of his time in his quarters due to never developing his sea legs. From the moment they left port, he felt nauseated, and walking the deck only made things worse. It was the only time in his life he avoided a strong drink; he wanted to keep himself from losing the contents of his stomach.

On what should have been one of the final nights among the waves, Rust went to the deck to retrieve a bucket. The crew's meat supply had started to turn, and already fighting the sea sickness, this was just what the dwarf needed to cause the bile to rise in his throat. He had not yet coughed up any sick, but it was only a matter of time.

While heading back to his quarters, Rust overheard a few of the sailors speaking in their bunks. By listening to what they were discussing, it was clear they thought everyone was asleep below deck.

"Captain pays us barely enough to get a woman port-side. Meanwhile, we got more riches aboard than any one man could spend in a lifetime."

"You're talking about a mutiny. They put men to death for less."

"I don't know about you, but I tire of making a peasant's wage."

"It's not only the captain we must worry about. What about that dwarf?"

Rust began to tip-toe to his quarters where his hammer was kept. Careful not to make any noise, he kept his ears open to hear more of the crew-members' plot.

"There's only one of him, and several of us. He gets in the way, he dies along with the captain."

The dwarf reached his door, and he slowly pushed it open, but nothing was going to stop the rusty hinges on the old ship from creaking loudly.

"What was that?" grumbled one of the sailors.

Before Rust could reach inside to the doorway where his hammer leaned against the wall, the footsteps of the crewmen rushing to the hallway could be heard on the wooden floor. Soon, the dwarf was looking at five of the nine seamen manning the ship.

"What are you doing sneaking around?" one asked.

"I was feeling sick," Rust said, lifting the bucket in his hand.

The crewmen all looked at one another, then finally came to a decision on what to do next as a sailor gave the order to, "Get him!"

The dwarf quickly ran into his room, and slammed his door, which caught one of the seamen in the face. This gave Rust enough time to grab the handle of his hammer and spin to build momentum. Just as the crewman pushed the door back open, the hammer struck him, caving his head in. He fell dead as the rest of the sailors tried to step over him, and enter the room.

After giving a loud, ear-piercing whistle, the dwarf swung the hammer down on one of their feet. The sound of breaking bone and wood could be heard, followed by a scream of pain. Rust then brought down his shoulder to push the man back out of his quarters, and into the three uninjured crewmen.

The sailors unsheathed their blades, and readied themselves for combat.

"Listen to me, dwarf," one of the seamen said. "We are armed and you are alone. Surrender and you will be spared. Perhaps richer. What say you?"

Rust had done many morally questionable things to get work, but when he took on a job for an employer, he was a dwarf of his word. Though the offer tempted him, it was only for a moment. Wealth was something he dreamed of, but not like this. Even if he did want to be part of his mutiny, it was too late anyway. He had already called for help.

"You will not defeat us," Rust announced. "Drop your swords, or we will be throwing your broken bodies overboard."

A crewman laughed, and asked, "What do you mean by us and we?"

Suddenly, the sound of hooves on wood came closer and closer. The sailors turned to the stairs leading to the deck to see Porter making haste down to the living quarters, still dragging the broken plank he'd been tied to at the ship's stables. Before they could raise their blades for an attack, the boar rammed the three crewmen with his massive tusks and his heavy hooves finished off the sailor shouting over his broken foot.

Rust came out of his quarters, and patted Porter on the nose saying, "That's a good boy."

The dwarf could see there was only one seaman with fight left in his body. As for the other two; one was disemboweled from a tusk and the other was unconscious. As the remaining crewman got to his feet, Rust put his head through a wall with a hard swing of his hammer.

It wasn't long before the captain made his way down to the living quarters to find out what all the chaos was about. Rust explained the sailors' plans, and a short interrogation of the unconscious crewman confirmed this. After the mutinous seaman's execution, the captain expressed his gratitude to the dwarf. However, with the number of his crew shrinking from nine to four, he needed Rust to pick up the workload.

For the remaining days at sea, the dwarf learned all he would need to know for keeping a ship afloat and moving. He had learned so quickly that he was offered a permanent position aboard the vessel. However, it turned out the dead sailors were right and the pay was too low. He could make what he was propositioned in only one job as a sellsword. Rust always thought what he learned while sweating on that cargo ship was something he would never use. This assumption would be proven wrong.

...

With the last rope removed, they were no longer connected to the pier. The mounts were secured in the small stable, and the redheaded dwarf ran to the mast to raise the main sail and jib. As the dwarven army closed in, the cloth caught the wind, moving the ship. Havish turned the wheel to guide them out to sea. After adjusting the boom, Rust tied the knots in the lines, and ran to assist the elf and half-elf in loading a bolt from the stack near the ballista.

The vessel had gotten some distance from the docks, but the bard noticed a flash of light in the thick, dark clouds nearby. This could only mean one thing, and Havish didn't need to have his sea legs to know it.

"Storm ahead!" the bard announced.

Rust looked out at open water to see lightning strike the waves, illuminating things enough to show the oncoming hard rain. He then checked behind him as one of the large dwarven warships' sails dropped. They were coming.

After a long string of obscenities, Rust cocked the ballista with the help of Saim.

"Fire at my signal," the dwarf ordered. "Havish, steer away from the storm."

"But we'll be going against the wind!" replied the bard.

"So be it!" cried Rust.

With the moist breeze in their faces, the warship was able to catch up to the travelers easily. Soon, they were close enough to hear the captain barking orders on the massive vessel's deck.

"Take aim at the sails!" commanded Rust.

Saim spun the crank on the side of the ballista to tilt the bolt upward. Meanwhile, Rust and Maurna turned the base of the weapon to face the oncoming ship.

"And," began the dwarf, waiting for the right moment, "fire!"

The half-elf pulled back the release lever, sending the projectile flying. The bolt whistled through the air as it headed toward the main sail on the gigantic warship. Unfortunately, the projectile barely missed its mark and splashed into the sea.

"Lower the aim!" barked Rust.

Before Saim could comply, the dwarf noticed a line of archers on the edge of the warship's deck. They all launched their arrows into the sky at the same time, stirring panic in the travelers.

"Down!" warned Rust.

Everyone on the small vessel ducked and covered their heads with their hands. Most of the arrows landed in the water, but a few stuck in the side of the hull and some landed upright in the deck.

Rust and Saim lifted a round into the ballista as Maurna spun the crank to lower the aim. As soon as they cocked the weapon, Maurna pulled the lever. The projectile again cut through the air with a high pitch, tore through the main sail, but did not slow the vessel.

After many loud clanks, bolts flew from the opposing ship. Most overshot the travelers, but one pierced the deck next to the stables. Porter and the two horses squealed in fear, but they were unharmed. Although the bolt was deep in the wood, they were in no danger of sinking, but it was only a matter of time. And it was clear that moment was not far away as the warship positioned itself in the water so the metal ram in the shape of a wolf pointed in the small vessel's direction.

"Reload!" Rust cried.

"No!" shouted Maurna. "It's hopeless!"

As Saim and the dwarf lifted another round onto the ballista, Rust cried out, "It's our only chance!"

"It's not!" she opposed. "Head into the storm!"

"Have you lost your mind!?!" questioned the dwarf. But as he looked at the staff in her hand, he realized her plan.

Rust turned to Havish and said, "You heard the elf! Into the storm!"

The bard spun the wheel and faced the ship toward the rain. With the sound of the wind whipping against the sails, they picked up speed, and just as the mage wanted, the warship followed.

A flash of the sky's wrath struck only a small distance from the front of the small vessel, where Maurna had positioned herself. The rain pattered on the deck as she looked to the opposing warship, which was preparing to ram. The mage raised her staff over her head and called upon the wind and water. A towering wave built near them, but it split around their vessel and struck the hull of their opponents.

The warship was forced a different direction, but the crew on the deck could be seen reloading their ballistas and the archers nocked arrows on their bows. After unleashing the projectiles toward the travelers, a strong gust of wet wind blew through. The arrows and bolts fell into the water, but more were coming.

Finally, Maurna shouted something in elvish into the black clouds, which crackled with shocking light. Then after pointing her staff at the warship, she repeated the incantation.

With precision, a bolt of lightning fell from the sky, striking the deck of the large vessel.

Wood splinters flew from the warship, and their sails caught aflame. The boat was motionless as the crewmen shouted in horror. Once the water below the vessel began bubbling, it was clear the ship was sinking.

Rust, Saim, and Havish cheered loud enough for the dwarves abandoning their vessel to hear them. The half-elf turned to Maurna at the front of their boat to praise her, but she was shivering, trying to hold herself up on all fours. The red-headed dwarf and the bard also noticed this, and their celebration instantly became concern.

Saim quickly ran to her and knelt down. She rolled into his arms with a groan as she tried to catch her breath. The half-elf moved the wet hair out of her eyes and shifted over her to block the rain.

"Maurna?" Saim's voice shook.

Her eyes finally opened a bit to meet his worried stare, and in a whisper she asked, "Are we safe?"

"We are," the half-elf sighed with relief. "Because of you. You saved us."

With a sleepy smile she could only say, "Good," and her eyes shut.

Fear came over Saim's face as Rust and Havish looked on sharing that same feeling. The half-elf lowered his scarred ear to her face to listen for breath, but the rain obscured his efforts. Then he saw her chest rise and fall. She was alive, but the fight had taken a lot out of her.

"She's going to be fine!" he informed the rest of the crew. Then returning his gaze to her, this time in an admiration he had never felt for anyone, he whispered to her, "We're all going to be fine."

Chapter XV

$\mathfrak{M}$aurna strolled through the forest, heading to the large trees forming the walls of Naughstaure. From here she could see the tall, natural watchtowers, and with the gentle calls from the birds around her, the elf felt safe. Unfortunately, this peacefulness wouldn't last long.

Suddenly, a screech echoed through the sky, which was slowly being darkened by thick, black clouds. The screams of her people swelled within the kingdom's walls, followed by the horns warning of the attack. Silhouettes of the winged beasts burst through the clouds, and swooped down into the kingdom.

The mage began to run to her troubled home, but no matter her pace or how many steps she took, it only seemed to get farther away. It wasn't until she saw smoke and the orange glow of flame that she realized it was hopeless. The sound of her people's cries silenced, leaving only the crackle of her smoldering home echoing in her ears. With an overwhelming sorrow in her heart, she fell to her knees, realizing that she had failed. Even in her dreams.

...

The weakened mage's eyes slowly opened to small beams of light shining through the small cracks in the wooden ceiling. She could hear water sloshing along the sides of the boat's hull around her. As she turned her head to examine her surroundings, she noticed Saim sitting on his bunk nearby.

"Maurna!" exclaimed the half-elf while rushing to her side. "How do you feel?"

Groggily she asked, "How long have I been asleep?"

"Three days."

The mage's eyes widened in shock, but the headache caused by her shrinking pupils made her wince. Saim quickly placed his hand gently on her forehead. He had never felt the flesh of an elf since his mother cradled him in his youth, but he could remember the race was not supposed to be so cold. He quickly grabbed a blanket, and threw it over her. She had never been in this helpless state before, so she grabbed the half-elf's arm to halt his kindness.

"You don't need to do that." she whimpered. "I'm fine."

"But you feel cold."

She struggled to sit up on the edge of her bunk, so Saim assisted by lifting Maurna by her shoulder. Too weak to fight him off, she placed her hand firmly on his chest. The half-elf stepped back, realizing he may be smothering her with his eagerness to help, but he was excited to see her wake from a sleep that he worried would never end.

"I'm sorry," he whispered.

"No," she began. "Thank you for your help."

Such simple words of gratitude had never felt as warm inside Saim's chest. They weren't even the kindest words he had heard from someone, but for reasons he couldn't explain, they felt more important.

"Have we had any trouble?" Maurna grumbled.

"The waters have been rough from time to time, but nothing we couldn't handle."

"Good."

The mage groaned as she attempted to push off her cot and stand on her shaking legs. Saim gently placed his hands under her forearm and on the small of her back to hold her steady, and even though she wanted to, she was too unstable on her feet to push the half-elf away.

"Take things slowly," the half-elf warned. "I don't want to cause more injury."

"Just take me above," she ordered, but realized immediately that her demands may be too harsh. "Please."

Saim nodded and slowly led her up the steps to the deck. She only had to shield her eyes for a moment in the daylight as her eyes adjusted. Framed by the clouds, the sun hovered over the horizon of the open sea. At the front of their tiny vessel, Havish played a slow, sad tune on his flute. A cool breeze blew through the sail and across the deck, which caused Maurna to shiver. The half-elf instantly pulled her closer to warm her, but she again held her hands against him to push him away.

"Are you sure you're going to be all right?" Saim asked.

She nodded and took a few slow, quivering steps away from him.

"There she is!" announced Rust as he stood behind the wheel steering the ship. "The one that pulled our rumps out of the fire. Glad to see you're awake."

Maurna looked at him and gave him a small smirk, then stumbled to the front of the ship.

Saim reached for her, but the dwarf stopped him by saying, "Let her go, boy. She's proven herself a strong one. She just needs her sea legs."

Saim agreed with this, but watched her to ensure that if she did fall, he could be there to catch her. Once Maurna reached the front of the vessel next to Havish, the half-elf decided to sit on one of the steps leading to the bridge. He moaned in exhaustion and took a deep breath of relief.

"Ah," said the bard as he halted his song, noticing the mage beside him. "Are you well?"

"Well enough," the mage grumbled as she leaned against the railing. "You can let that abomination know that he need not be so concerned for me."

"That *abomination* hasn't left your side from the moment you closed your eyes. Not even to eat."

"He didn't eat?" she scoffed. "How foolish of him."

"I thought that as well, until I asked why."

"And his reason?"

"He knew you didn't pack any food for this journey, and he wanted to ensure that you had some when you awoke. The lad felt the need to check on you so often, he didn't even sleep."

Maurna looked back at the half-elf, who had already lowered his head in an exhausted sleep. Unaware, a smile forced its way across her face. She may have disapproved of all the attention her state had caused her, but the elf had never seen this much worry from anyone other than Faylin.

"Why?" she wondered aloud.

"We are all thankful for your aid," explained Havish, "but that half-elf's heart is so full, despite the prejudice of humans and your people alike. It's a curiosity to me, but I'd say he feels more than gratitude for your assistance. I'd say he favors you quite a bit."

"What do you mean by that?"

"Play coy if you must, but you know exactly what I mean."

With that, the bard put his flute to his lips and played an old tune he hadn't played since he was a young man. It was one of the first songs he had ever learned, but he hadn't felt the urge to play it again until this moment. It was an intoxicating melody, which caused Maurna to stare at the dozing Saim, and ponder her own bigotry.

The farther south the ship sailed, the warmer the air became. Muggy humidity from the seas made the weather feel even hotter and stickier.

Over the next days, the travelers had shed most of their clothing. Saim, Maurna, and Havish had kept their modesty as much as they could tolerate, but Rust had not worn a shirt since the temperatures started to rise. The bard, half-elf, and mage often questioned this, because his race was naturally resistant to heat. However, they didn't dare say anything to the dwarf, knowing the confined space of their ship was causing tensions to be high enough.

They would sleep in shifts, using the position of the sun to dictate the hours. The fortunate thing about this stolen vessel was that Runehelm had not only stocked it with ammunition for the ballista, but had also stored bread, meat, and fresh water.

It was assumed this boat must have been frequently used by the dwarves for patrols. With the hardships the travelers had endured thus far, this was seen as lucky. To Maurna it was seen as a gift provided by the Great Spirit. The heat too was a blessing in disguise, because it meant they were nearly to their destination in the Southern Continent.

To fight the high temperatures, and the bodily odors, the travelers would collect sea water to soak their clothing and wash themselves. The salt content of the ocean wasn't a very effective means for bathing, but it was either that or nothing. The only other water available was for drinking, and that would just be a careless waste to use.

One quiet night, after about six long hours of steering the ship with Saim, Maurna sent him below to wake Havish and Rust for their shift. After only a few moments, Havish emerged from the sleeping quarters, wiping his eyes.

He slowly walked up the steps to the bridge saying, "Rest up. I'll take over from here."

The elf let go of the wheel and stepped aside to let the bard steer. She stretched her back and headed to the edge of the boat to lower a bucket into the sea. After collecting some water, she pulled the bucket back up, untied it from the rope, and headed to the sleeping quarters.

Her eyes were already having trouble staying open, but once she entered the sleeping quarters they opened wide in surprise. Saim sat on his bunk, facing away from the stairwell where the elf stood. His shirt was laying beside him, and he was dipping a cloth into a bucket of sea water. He used the cloth to wipe his neck, letting the drops cascade down his back.

True the mage was female, and noticed the half-elf's build was impressive, but what really caught her eye was the many scars along his shoulders. Beyond her natural urges of reproduction, something inside her also felt pity. She had never felt either of those things about something spawned by a human.

Saim turned, saw her gawking at him, and instantly felt self-conscious.

Hastily, he put his shirt back on, saying, "Maurna, my apologies. I didn't know you'd be down here so quickly."

"That isn't necessary," she replied as she continued to her cot. "Continue."

The half-elf watched her sit and place her bucket of sea water on the floor beside her. She was no longer looking at him, but he still felt too embarrassed to keep his shirt off.

"I assure you," she muttered, "you need not feel shamed for anything."

"What of my scars?" he asked. "Do they not disgust you?"

"What of mine?" she said, motioning to the mark along her cheek.

"Nothing about you disgusts me."

Maurna met his eyes with a grin and reddened face, mumbling, "Nor does anything about you."

Both Saim and the mage sat in a bashful silence, until Rust, in his bunk, groaned, "Can you two keep it down?"

"Don't you have a ship to sail?" hissed Maurna in frustration.

"Aye," the dwarf answered, sitting up from his cot. "I suppose I do."

Rust yawned, got to his feet, and picked up his shirt as if to put it on over his bare chest, but instead used it to wipe the sweat from his brow. He threw the shirt to the ground, coughed, spit, and after picking up his hammer, he walked slowly to the steps leading to the upper deck.

Before leaving, he turned to the mage and half-elf to say, "Rest well. We'll be arriving at the Southern Continent in only a day."

Soon, Rust was out of sight, leaving Saim and Maurna alone. For a while, they tried to act as if they were by themselves. The mage dipped a cloth in the bucket, and began to wipe it along her chest and neck. This seemed to mesmerize the half-elf as he pretended not to stare, watching a few drops fall from shoulders to the top of her breast.

Finally, Maurna broke the silence. "Would you mind if I asked you something?"

Saim looked away and replied, "No."

"Those scars. How did you get them?"

"I've had them for as long as I can remember," he explained. "It was a long time ago. I was still just a boy. Sailing along the seas with pirates."

...

The morning after the voices of the dragons and abysmyths told Separ the key leading to the Door of Sight Unseen was within his own son, he decided to immediately find out how. The captain pulled the child away from his screaming mother with the help of two crewmen, and took him to the bowels of the ship.

Though Saim was still just a child, the Dragon's Voice would not stop the interrogation till he found answers.

"I know you have it, boy," growled Separ in a deep, raspy voice, "and one way or another, I will take it."

Young Saim hadn't a clue what the captain meant, so he remained frozen in silent fear. The Dragon's Voice saw the fright in the quivering child, and lifted his eye patch to reveal the mangled flesh that had healed around the Eye of Sight Unseen in the left socket. Separ assumed the red jewel would be able to see the small half-elf and the whispers in his mind would tell him how this boy had the key. But it was silent.

Frustrated, the captain grabbed Saim's throat and whispered, "I will have the key. Even if I have to pull you apart to get it."

He threw the young half-elf to the floor then walked to the wall where a thin leather strap hung off a hook. Just as the child tried to pick himself up off the floor, Separ walked back with the strap in hand. After kicking Saim's hands out from under him, the captain leaned over and held the boy's wrists above his head. Then with the other hand, the Dragon's Voice whipped the leather across the half-elf's back.

Saim cried out in pain and tried to struggle out of Separ's grasp, but he was much too large and much too strong for the child. Soon the strap began to break through the boy's skin. A few more strikes, and the child went numb, too exhausted to sob or fight any longer. His tears rolled from his eyes and made a pool under his face.

Finally, the beating ceased, and Separ got to his feet, out of breath, saying, "You're still alive. Next time, you may not be so fortunate."

The child kept his head against the floor, unable to gather the strength to move. All he could do was listen to the captain's footsteps as he walked to the table in the room. Separ grabbed a bottle of rum sitting atop a barrel and pulled out the cork using his teeth. Once he spit the cork across the room, he took a couple of gulps of the brown liquid.

After swallowing, the Dragon's Voice groaned, "I can make this pain last much longer than you can keep a secret. Remember that."

With that, the captain turned the bottle upside down, pouring the rest of the bottle on little Saim's open wounds. The boy opened his mouth to gasp for breath, and once he filled his lungs, he used it all to howl in agony.

...

After hearing the story of Saim's scars, Maurna fell silent, only shaking her head in a saddened disbelief. She had never thought of what kind of life a half-elf would have to endure. Unable to find a place in the world. Rejected by everyone.

Saim didn't like being pitied, and from her silence, he could tell that's what was happening. He quickly changed the subject with the question, "How about you?"

She looked up at him, snapping out of her thoughts.

"Your scar," he clarified. "How did it happen?"

"It happened when I was training my ability," she explained. "I had ventured too far outside the Naughstaure forest. A couple of bandits tried to have their way with me. When I struggled, one cut me with his dagger."

"I'm sorry," Saim whispered. "Were they human?"

"Yes."

"Did they—?"

"No," she said with a smirk. "In all the panic, I prayed to the Great Spirit. Before I knew it, limbs from the trees wrapped around their necks. They were lifted away from me, and they were strangled to death."

"The Great Spirit?" he repeated. "One could argue it was your ability that saved you."

"Yes, but it was He who gave me this gift."

Saim nodded in agreement, and he mumbled, "Now I see why you dislike humans so. And me."

"It's true that humans killed my parents, and scarred me. This caused me much distaste for their kind. It is also true that when I first met you, I felt nothing but hatred. But I've seen that I was wrong to feel this way."

"You have?" the half-elf asked, trying not to look too eager for approval, but it was difficult considering he hadn't had it since childhood.

"I have," she laughed. "However, you're not only human. You are also elf."

"Not quite," Saim sighed, pulling his hair back to reveal his mangled ear, "I'm like you said. An abomination."

"Ears don't make someone an elf. It's your soul. Abominations don't have them. And over the course of our travels, I have seen yours."

The half-elf felt his cheeks go warm, and he looked away. Only one elf had ever made him feel so important, but she was gone. He remembered how tightly she would embrace him after telling him how special he was, and something inside Saim wanted to share that experience with Maurna.

When he looked back up, the mage was no longer sitting on her bunk, but on his. She bashfully looked at her hands as the half-elf stared at her.

"Havish told me what you did for me while I was asleep," she said, "and I just wanted to give you my thanks."

He had never been this close to a female. Not like this. Not the way she looked at him. And not the way it made him feel.

"You're welcome," he whispered, keeping his eyes locked on her.

Abruptly, Havish ran down the stairs leading to the sleeping quarters, shouting, "Saim! Maurna! Awaken!"

The elf and half-elf stood looking in the direction of the clamoring to see the bard in a panic.

"What is it?" asked Maurna.

"We've a problem!" Havish's voice shook.

Before another question could be asked, the sound of a distant screech could be heard. They knew the sound, for they had heard it many times before. More wails from the dragons rang out, but this time slightly closer.

The bard stared at Saim and Maurna with his eyes widening to mumble the obvious statement, "They found us."

Chapter XVI

Havish ran out of the sleeping quarters, followed by Saim and Maurna, weapons in hand. Rust held the wheel but didn't seem too focused on the waters ahead. His eyes squinted into the night sky behind the small ship, and he trapped his breath into his lungs to listen closer.

As the bard, half-elf, and mage darted up the steps to the bridge, the dwarf held up his hand to silence them. They froze in their place and looked out into the dark.

Suddenly, the sound of danger echoed, but it was much too dark to see how close it was. Then, directly in the light of the moon, the form of the scaly, winged creature showed itself. Then another. Then eight more.

The fleet of dragons flew in a V formation with men upon their backs, and they were coming straight for the small vessel. It would only be a matter of minutes before they were in range of attack.

"Battle stations!" cried Rust.

Instantly, Havish ran up the stairs to steer the boat while Saim and the dwarf rushed to load a bolt into the ballista. Maurna stood on the back of the bridge and readied her staff. Rust cocked the ballista as the half-elf turned the crank to raise the aim. After turning the ballista in the direction of the oncoming threat, all was quiet.

"Steady," Rust said.

Only the sounds of the water along the sides of the hull, the distant groaning of the onslaught, the travelers' shallow breaths, and the mage's whispered prayers to the Great Spirit were all that could be heard.

"Steady."

Each of them felt as if their heart would pound through their chest, and they shook with anticipation.

"Steady."

They were at the mercy of the waves and any deity that existed.

"Steady!"

Skill alone could not save them.

"Hold!"

The jewel on the mage's staff began to glow, and as she waved it in the air, the water around the boat began to swell in a wave. Saim pulled an arrow from his quiver, and pulled it back on his bow.

"Hold!"

Just then, the dragons broke formation, and swooped low to swarm the ship.

"Now!" screamed Rust as he fired the ballista.

The bolt wailed through the air toward a cluster of the monsters, but the beasts darted out of the way. The half-elf let go of his arrow, which buried itself into the scales of one of the dragons' legs. It didn't deter the monster in the least.

One dragon swooped across the bow of the vessel, spraying fire along the wooden boards, which instantly ignited. The fire spread, inching closer to the stables.

"Forget the wheel!" the dwarf shouted to Havish. "Man the ballista!"

Rust darted to the stable with his hammer over his head as the bard left the wheel and rushed to the ballista. The dwarf reached the stable and smashed the lock on the door. The wood splintered, freeing Lurya, Porter, and Havish's horse just as the stable began to catch fire.

Havish loaded a bolt into the ballista, aimed it at one of the flying beasts, and fired it. The dragon didn't turn in time to see the projectile speeding toward it, and it impaled its torso. The monster fell from the sky, throwing the pirate on its back into the sea as it skid along the top of the water.

Another dragon tried to swoop back across the bow of the ship, but Maurna sent a wall of waves in front of it. After hitting the barrier of water, the beast spun out of control. As it went down into the sea, the swashbuckler on its back leapt off his mount and landed on the deck. Before he could get to his feet, Rust used his weapon to crush the pirate's skull against the wooden floor.

As the water from the conjured wave fell onto the boat, the flames on the deck extinguished. Meanwhile, Saim readied another arrow, and Havish loaded another bolt. As the bard cocked the ballista, the half-elf managed to take down the drag-on he had previously wounded with a well-placed arrow to the ribs.

Havish fired at an approaching monster, but it maneuv-ered out of the way and dove to land atop the ballista. The bard fell backward as the large weapon collapsed under the beast's weight. As the dragon brought its head back to take in a breath, Havish scrambled to his feet and pulled his sword. Before it could bring its head down to spew forth its fire, the bard dragged his blade along the creature's throat.

Blood and flammable fluid poured from the monster's open wound. Havish jumped back as fire spread on the floorboards at his feet. As the beast's head fell limp onto the deck, the pirate upon its back ran down its neck with his sword held over his head. The bard quickly blocked the sword, grabbed the buccaneer's collar, and threw him down into the crackling fire. Before the pirate could pull his own burning body out of the flame, Havish stuck him with his blade, finishing him.

As a dragon sped toward the vessel, Maurna called upon another large wave to pull it out of the sky. The beast went down, but struck the hull with a mighty force. Boards gave into the pressure of the creature's body and snapped, sending sea water into the sleeping quarters. The ship was going down.

The mage's eyes widened at the heavy damage to the vessel, but Saim, Havish, and Rust were too busy fighting off the remaining swarm that was latching onto the side of the ship. As the beasts blew fire toward the travelers and their mounts on the deck, the pirates hopped off their dragons and landed onboard.

The dwarf did his best to fight off the two men attacking him, but he was tiring out. The bard also had two buccaneers on the offensive, and even his skill alone couldn't stand up to the numbers. The sound of metal-on-metal melee was only a whisper compared to the creaking and snapping of the wood planks that the dragons were pulling off the vessel.

A winged creature had perched itself behind Maurna, but she was so distracted by the commotion of their defeat, she didn't notice. The beast roared as it lunged at her, but before it could sink its teeth into her, an arrow landed in the monster's neck. After a screech of pain, the dragon took back to the sky. The mage looked to the half-elf, who was pulling another arrow from his quiver and running up the steps to the bridge.

Suddenly, the wood below the water gave out, shifting the ship backward. Unable to keep balance, everyone onboard fell to the floor. The pirates scrambled to their feet, and darted back to their dragons. Once on the beasts' backs, they took flight again, leaving the travelers to their sinking vessel.

"Saim!" Maurna cried. "We're sinking!"

Before the half-elf could respond, more boards snapped, causing the bridge to dip into the water. The mage began to slide toward the water, so she used her staff to hook around some of the loose planks. When the boards started to pull away from the floor, she screamed in fear.

"Hold on!" Saim cried as he stumbled to get his footing.

He ran to her aid, careful not to fall down the incline. Finding it impossible to keep his footing, he gripped the wheel on the bridge and extended his bow toward Maurna.

"Grab it!" he shouted.

The bow was just slightly out of reach, and she stretched out her arm as far as she could. Touching the bow with the tips of her fingers, she could almost get a grip on it. She strained to reach farther with a groan deep from her throat, as if to tell the Great Spirit this was not where she would die.

She looked into Saim's eyes with desperation as she saw a dragon swooping down toward the half-elf. She tried to warn him by screaming, "Saim!"

It was too late. The beast wrapped its clawed hand around the half-elf, and pulled him into the sky. He struggled to get out of the monster's grasp, but it was no use. The creature was too strong.

"No!" Maurna cried out.

With Saim in its grasp, the dragon and the rest of the winged creatures took to the air and instantly flew away from the sinking ship. In a matter of seconds, the beasts were gone.

More boards snapped, breaking the vessel in half, sending Havish, Rust, and the mage into the water. Their mounts were still aboard the half of the ship still afloat, but it wouldn't be for much longer. The remaining travelers grabbed floating boards, while spitting the splashing sea water out of their mouths. Other than the few corpses in the water, Maurna, the dwarf, and the bard were alone. Once the remainder of the ship sank, their mounts would be among the floating dead.

Just when it seemed to be the end, the water began to become unsteady. Waves built around the travelers, making it difficult for them to hold their heads above the sea.

Suddenly, the water began to swirl around them. It was as if the sea was swallowing them up. Havish and Maurna would have tried to fight the current like Rust was futilely trying, but they were much too defeated to care. They had failed, so as far as they were concerned, the water could have them.

It wasn't long before the sea had become a spiral of waves, sucking down the bard, dwarf, mage, the bodies of the dead, and the remains of the small ship with Havish's horse, Lurya, and Porter aboard. All that were still alive shrieked in fear, wondering how things could get worse, yet positive it was about to, they took one final breath, and sank below the waves.

...

Saim struggled to get out of the dragon's grasp for what felt like an eternity, but every time he felt he had almost freed himself, the beast tightened its grip. Even if he were to escape the dragon, he only had the endless sea to catch his fall. Along with the certainty that his friends were dead, he really had no reason to fight any longer, so he finally gave up.

In a few moments, a large vessel peeked over the dark watery horizon. Massive and countless black sails carried a ship covered in iron armor. A steel dragon ram decorated the front of the boat, and even from the great distance, Saim could see stables where the real dragons were landing and being kept. Something about this vessel seemed a bit familiar to the half-elf. He had seen this ship before, but he was much too young when he had last laid eyes on it. Though he was certain of whose ship this was.

As the dragon carrying him came closer to the boat, Saim saw the many pirates running all around the vessel like scattering insects. They cried out in a victorious celebration as they saw their men coming back with their captive. This was salt in the half-elf's wounds. It further reminded the half-elf of his failure. Everything was lost. The enemy had won.

The winged beast had finally reached the vessel, and it hovered over the bridge of the ship, slowly lowering itself to the stables. Then when it was at man's height, it dropped Saim onto the deck. The half-elf slammed hard on his stomach against the wooden floor as the dragon landed nearby at the stables. The pirate climbed off his creature's back, instantly praised for his triumph by his fellow crewmen.

Saim groaned as swashbucklers gathered around him. After trying to pick himself up, the buccaneers all took turns kicking and stomping his ribs. Saim curled into a ball, trying to block himself from the beating, but the pain was becoming so unbearable that he started to lose consciousness.

Suddenly, the attack stopped as a deep voice ordered, "Enough!"

The pirates parted to let the person who had given the order through the crowd. The boards moaned under the weight of the large man's boots. Saim's eyes were blurred from the shock of the beating, and all he could see was the tanned, leathery skin of the bald captain. He had aged since the half-elf had last seen him, and the scar peeking out of his eye patch had hardened as well. But there was no doubt in Saim's mind about who this was.

"Son," grumbled Separ, "it has been too long."

Chapter XVII

Maurna, Rust, and Havish coughed, trying to get out the bit of sea water that had made it into their lungs. After finally being able to catch a breath, they looked around at their surroundings. Things were brighter here than on the surface of the sea. The question of whether or not they were dead went through all their minds. However, the dwarf just wanted to know one thing.

"Porter?" Rust cried out as his eyes darted around the room. "Porter!"

A squeal was heard from the ship rubble nearby. The dwarf got to his feet, and darted to the broken vessel where Porter climbed out of the broken wood. Rust wrapped his arms around the boar's neck. It was obvious both were ecstatic to see one another alive.

Havish's horse and Lurya emerged unscathed from the splintered boards as well. Somehow, everyone had survived, but no one could think of how or why they were saved. They also couldn't seem to figure out where they were, considering they had seen nothing like it before.

The room was spherical on top, and flat on bottom with a pool of water in the center of the floor. On closer inspection, it wasn't a pool. It was an opening to the sea, which they were surrounded by. The room was a clear enclosure, allowing them to look out into the water where several different fish swam in schools, curiously looking inward at the travelers.

"Where are we?" asked Maurna.

Havish could only shake his head in a speechless uncertainty.

Suddenly, they could see human-shaped lifeforms swimming under the enclosure toward the opening in the floor. The travelers would have been threatened by the arrival of these things, but it seemed as if they were responsible for saving their lives.

The first four of these beings leapt from the water onto the floor of the enclosure with jagged spears in hand that appeared to be made of stone and coral. The same material made up the armor covering the creature's shoulders, chest, forearms, thighs, and shins. They had the pointed ears of an elf, but the gills and webbed digits of a sea dweller. Their skin was a bluish hue, which was almost transparent, showing the veins moving a blue blood glowing with wisps of white through their bodies.

Jewels lined their wet hairline, and corners of their armor. It was clear these were soldiers.

They spoke, pointing their spears, but it wasn't a language recognized by Rust. It was an accent not heard before, but Maurna and Havish knew it was still elvish. The soldiers were asking that they remove all weapons, but Maurna informed them they did not have any due to losing them in a pirate attack. Her staff, the dwarf's hammer, and the bard's sword were somewhere on the bottom of the sea.

After looking the travelers up and down, the soldiers finally lowered their spears, calling out the elven word for *safe*. After that, another of the beings slowly lifted from the pool of water. Once he was level with the floor, he stepped out of the pool. His armor had long cloth draping off of it like a robe, and instead of a spear, he carried a staff made from coral. On the top was a blue jewel, shining like the sun reflecting off of the sea.

The robed being walked to Maurna as he slowly extended his hand to her face. Panic began to swell within her, so Havish ordered him to stop in his elven tongue. The being turned to the bard, and explained in his native words that he meant no harm. Then the being turned back to the elf, and gently placed his hand on her forehead. For a moment she looked confused, but suddenly she gasped. It wasn't pain. It was surprise.

After only a few seconds, the being brought his hand away leaving a blue hand print on her forehead. As the hand print faded away, the blue person spoke.

"Water is the core element of every living thing. With it, we are able to have an understanding with all creatures. I am Morst. General mage of the Earenthall army."

"What are you?" Rust blurted out.

"Long ago, when the war ended between the humans and elves, we are the ones who found our home underwater," informed the blue elf. "The Great Spirit helped us adapt to our new environment, and in return we guard the sea."

"I've heard stories," Maurna uttered. "I thought that's all they were."

"Why did you save us?" Havish asked.

"We thought we were under attack," replied Morst. "The waves were causing quite the disturbance. We didn't realize it was one of our kind."

"My apologizes," uttered the elf.

"Not necessary," said the sea-mage, "But it was you under attack?"

"Pirates," began the dwarf. "They sank us. Captured one of our people."

"We have dealt with their kind before," grumbled Morst. "It is I who am sorry for your loss."

"Perhaps you could help us," mentioned the bard.

"I fear I cannot answer you," said the sea-elf, "for it is not I who can make such decisions."

"And who can?" Maurna asked.

"Come," ordered Morst as he walked to the curved wall of the enclosure. He placed his hand on the surface, and it opened up a transparent tunnel that led out of the room.

"Where are we going?" pondered Havish aloud.

Morst turned to the travelers with a smile and said, "We are going to find out if we can assist you. We are going to meet with our king."

With that, the travelers, their mounts, and the soldiers followed the general mage out of the enclosure, and into the clear tunnel.

...

Saim was still fighting for consciousness as the pirates threw him in the lower part of the ship. Bruised and bleeding, the half-elf lay on the wooded floorboards, dripping crimson from his mouth. Separ walked to his motionless body, knelt down, and lifted his head by his hair to meet his half-opened eyes.

"I hope you won't die as easily as your mother, boy," the captain grumbled. "I need you alive."

Saim was only able to groan in his defense, which made the Dragon's Voice smile. He let go of the half-elf's hair, letting his head limply fall to the wooden ground. Then he stood and sauntered to the reinforced door.

Before shutting the door, he said to his crewmen, "We no longer need the elf. See that he is dead before we reach the Southern Continent."

As the door slammed and Saim heard the lock clang into place, he could only wonder what the captain meant. If the half-elf weren't broken in both body and spirit, he would have tried to figure it out and would have tried to find a way to escape, but there was nothing left to fight for. Nothing at all. Not even the world.

"They caught you," uttered a voice in the dark bowels of the ship. "I guess all is truly lost."

It was a familiar voice, which caused enough curiosity to inspire Saim to move. He could only muster the energy to slide his face on the ground so he could glance at the source of the voice.

Faylin, the king of the former Naughstaure, sat against the wall with tattered clothing and blackened bruises on his face. It was clear he had been efficiently abused in the days since the fall of his kingdom due to his malnourished physique.

"I must admit," the former elven king whimpered, "it is nice to see a friendly face."

...

Shortly after Faylin admitted his betrayal to the Elven Elders of Naughstaure, they immediately stripped him of his crown, and sentenced him to death. He went from king to enemy of his kingdom in only one night. Faylin had only a day to make peace with the Great Spirit, and would be decapitated first thing the next morning. Knowing that he had acted within the will of the Great Spirit without remorse, he used the remainder of his time in the world to pray for Maurna's safety as she led the travelers to the Door of Sight Unseen.

The fact that his life had a limit made the time seem to fly by. Before he knew it, guards arrived to the tree-giant, and his cell hovering above the kingdom lowered to the ground. Once the cage was opened, the soldiers led Faylin to the center of Naughstaure, where a tall boulder stained with the blood of elven criminals and human intruders sat. The guards threw him against the stone, and instantly roots grew from the ground, wrapping around his wrists. With his hands bound, the roots forced his arms open across the large rock. His back was pressed firmly against the rock as he looked out into the faces of the elves he had once led that were gathering to watch the death of a traitor.

Suddenly, the horns of the kingdom's army blared to let the people know of the king's imminent death. Then the whispering voices of the Elders boomed through Naughstaure in the native tongue. They announced that on this morning, they were executing the once-mighty king and the crowd cheered as tears rolled from Faylin's eyes, not because this would be his last sunrise, but because the people he loved would so easily cast him out. Though he was accused of being a traitor, at this moment, he was the one who felt betrayed.

The Elders continued to list his crimes against the kingdom. He had admitted guilt to going against commands of the Great Spirit, conspiring to release prisoners of the kingdom, and aiding the pirate Separ. To this the crowd hissed, and spit at the once-king's feet.

With the list of his crimes complete, the Elders asked him if he had anything to say before his demise. With a quivering voice of fear and sadness, he only said that it was easy for the Elders to make judgments, locked away from the world, because they would never have to deal with the consequences. Faylin went on to say the word of the Elders was not the word of the Great Spirit, only their interpretation. The Great Spirit would never wish death. Not on man, beast, elf, or what the elves deemed as an abomination. The Great Spirit is a being of love, creation, and love for His creations. Faylin claimed he was doing only what he thought was beneficial for all living things, and he did not regret this. If he was wrong, the Great Spirit would forgive him, and gladly accept him into His paradise.

The elves voiced their disapproval, and demanded the blasphemer be put to death. Pushing his way through the crowd, the executioner made his way to the execution stone. The former king watched as he turned to the audience and lifted his ceremonial and ornate two handed ax over his head. The people of Naughstaure cheered with joy.

The next moments seemed to go much too slowly as the elated chants of the elves began to be drowned out by Faylin's anticipation. Tears in his eyes made it harder to see his executioner walk closer and closer. Once in striking distance, the ax was lifted. The former king shut his eyes, and prepared to meet the Great Spirit in person.

Suddenly, the tallest tree in Naughstaure burst into flames as a ball of fire fell from the sky. This was followed by a storm of fiery rain hitting the rest of the wooden towers and homes. The elven settlers instantly began to panic and run for cover. Faylin wondered if this was divine intervention of the Great Spirit, but then he saw the winged beasts dive down into the kingdom.

As a dragon landed within the walls of the kingdom, the executioner ran to fight for his home and with only one breath of fire, the beast set the executioner aflame. The ax flew from his burning hands, and landed at the former king's feet.

Faylin quickly struggled to pull the weapon closer with his feet, as the dragon walked toward him. Panicked, he got his foot under the blade, and kicked it up to lean against his side. The sharp edge sliced him slightly, but he was much too focused to care. He nudged it with his hip, and it managed to fall into his grasp. After checking to see how close the dragon was, he could see the beast was raising its head to take in a deep breath. Faylin used his limited movement to saw through the root that bound his hands to the stone. Just as the monster lowered its mouth to spew flame, the former king freed his wrist and spun behind the large rock.

Fire flew around the boulder, leaving Faylin unharmed. Once the flames ended, the former king cut his other hand free. Before he could retreat, the dragon peered over the top of the stone. Faylin quickly swung the ax, planting it firmly into the skull of the beast. In its last movement, it jerked its head back, pulling the ax from the king's grasp. He would have gone to retrieve the weapon, but when he looked out from behind the large rock, he saw that more winged beasts had landed, and pirates were climbing off of their backs.

Faylin ran in the opposite direction toward the walls surrounding Naughstaure, as the sound of his people screaming echoed in his ears. He still managed to feel pity for them despite their lust for his blood, but old habits die hard. Now, so must he.

Just before he reached the wall, a dragon landed in front of him with such force it shook Faylin off his feet. He scooted himself backward as the beast approached with a laughing swashbuckler on its back.

Another winged monster landed behind the king, and the pirate on his back shouted, "Not this one! Separ will want him alive!"

More of the buccaneers had found their way to Faylin with their blades ready for an attack. There were far too many for the king to fight, so he got to his knees, and lowered his head in defeat. With his surrender, the pirates tied him to one of their beasts, and took him away from his burning kingdom to the bowels of Separ's ship.

...

"I never told them the plan," assured Faylin. "The Elders told them before they were burned alive. They kept me, so if Maurna were found, they could buy her loyalty with my life. I assured them it wouldn't work, but they kept me here regardless."

Saim pulled himself to the wall with a moan and leaned against the wood, holding his ribs. He spit the blood from his mouth, but the taste of copper lingered.

"Is she still alive?" asked the former king.

The half-elf was sure the sea had taken Maurna's life, but he still responded with, "I can't be certain."

"So perhaps not all is lost."

Faylin's faith still had some fight left, but Saim knew nothing could save them. They were doomed and so was this world.

...

It seemed the transparent tunnel would never end as Havish, his horse, Rust, Maurna, Porter, Lurya, Morst, and his guards walked through it. Though the view from inside the sea was beautiful, there was a rescue to attend to.

Finally, the tunnel ended and they arrived at the magnificently large castle carved out of stone and coral. Glowing orbs lit the way to the massive doors, which had more guards around it. It too was surrounded in a clear enclosure, allowing the viewing of all the sea creatures swimming around it.

It wasn't much longer before they were entering the castle to see the inside was just as impressive. Straight ahead was a throne growing from the floor of the great hall, and upon that throne was the king, surrounded by more of his guards. Behind him was a window into the sea, where blue-elves could be seen attaching armor to a plethora of underwater creatures. Whales, sharks, mammoth crabs, and giant squids waited patiently as the stone and coral was strapped to their flesh and shells.

The king looked at the approaching travelers, their mounts, his general mage, and his guards, asking in elvish if the unexpected guests were the cause of the disturbance to their waters. Before Morst could answer, Havish spoke up in their tongue to explain that they were attacked. This impressed the king, but he wondered if all could speak the language. Maurna looked to Rust, and shook her head, so he motioned for his general to come closer. Once Morst had climbed up the few steps to the throne, the king placed his hand on his forehead.

In moments he removed his hand, turned to the travelers, and said, "I am Vawn. I welcome you to my kingdom. Though I wish it was under better circumstances."

"As do I," the bard agreed. "This is why I must request your aid."

The king sighed and uttered, "I understand you have lost much, and for that we can return you to the shore. But as for rescuing the lost member of your party, we cannot help. Our people do not mettle in the affairs of the surface."

"They were pirates!" shouted Rust. "Your general said you had problems with them before!"

"That may be," grumbled Vawn, "but the only ship in our waters was yours. To go out of our boundaries, and attack a vessel would be breaking our promise to the Great Spirit. We are duty-bound to protect this place, and nothing more."

"You foolish bottom-feeders!" the dwarf cried out. "Does everyone we meet have to be this selfish!?!"

"Rust!" Havish scolded before pleading, "This is no ordinary pirate ship. It is commanded by Separ. The Dragon's Voice."

"I have heard of this man," Morst spoke up. "He seeks the Door of Sight Unseen. Does he not?"

"He does," the dwarf mumbled. "He has the key. A member of our crew. And it's my fault."

The bard and Maurna turned to Rust with confusion.

"What do you mean?" asked Havish.

The dwarf reluctantly explained, "When we first met back in that town, a pirate asked if I had seen someone by your description after you left. I told him where to find you, so that I could rescue you and you'd hire me. But I didn't realize what kind of danger you were in, or the severity of—"

The bard silenced Rust by striking him with a balled-up fist. The sea-elf guards grabbed Havish and pulled him away from the dwarf shouting for him to stop in their native tongue.

"How could you?" whispered Maurna in disbelief. "We trusted you, and you didn't feel it necessary to tell us this."

"I didn't feel I needed to," grumbled the dwarf as he spit blood from his mouth. "Not until I arrived at Runehelm. I have done a lot of selfish things I need to pay for, and I'm trying my best to make up for them."

The bard fought to get free screaming, "You are the reason they were able to follow us to Naughstaure! It was by your hand that it was destroyed, and you have kept Separ on our heels! If Saim is dead, trust that I will ensure you join him!"

"If that is the case," Rust began getting to his feet, "I will not fight you."

"Enough!" ordered Vawn. "Now, I wish we could assist you further, but the actions of the Dragon's Voice do not affect Earenthall."

"Does it not?" Maurna asked, approaching the king. "One elven kingdom has already been turned to rubble. How long before it's yours?"

"I am sorry to hear that," the king replied. "But the loss of one kingdom does not warrant a pattern."

"Nothing is sacred to this pirate!" Rust grumbled with blood running from his lip, "And once he opens the Door of Sight Unseen, he will use the power he finds inside to make this world his own. He will come here, and he will take your lives."

Vawn had always heard stories of how no human or dwarf was to be trusted, but the sincerity he heard in their voices seemed to prove this theory wrong. In his tongue, he asked his guards to release the bard and ordered Havish to come closer.

Once at the throne, the king said, "I understand the dwarf would like to redeem himself, and the land-elf would like revenge against this pirate. But you, Havish, speak with so much more passion than just a man who wants to save the world. I must see your true motivation."

The bard nodded, and bowed toward the king. Vawn placed his hand on Havish's forehead. Instantly, a cold rush went through his brow, and he felt as if the king had asked more questions than he could answer as every inch of the bard's mind was searched. Every memory, no matter how distant, or secret, no matter how small, was revealed to the sea-elf.

Finally, Vawn moved his hand away, and uttered, "I see."

As the blue hand print faded on Havish's forehead, he asked once more, "Will you help us?"

The king squinted as he thought of his response. Maurna, the bard, his horse, Rust, Porter, Lurya, and Morst waited for his decision in a silent anticipation that sent chills through their bodies. Finally, Vawn sighed as a smile crossed his face.

"Earenthall is at your side. What do you request of us?"

Chapter XVIII

ountless hours had gone by as Saim and Faylin sat
in the holding cell in the bowels of the old, creaking pirate ship.
They were much too injured to make any conversation, and were
completely unaware that a day had passed. The former king
spent most of his time fighting for consciousness, but when sleep
took over, he mumbled incoherently. The half-elf was positive
Faylin was dreaming, and could only think of what a horrible
thing it must have been to have a nightmare only to wake up to
another.

As the sun began setting outside, their cell door flew
open, and two buccaneers stormed in. Without a word, they
instantly grabbed the former king's arms and pulled him to the
door. Saim attempted to get up to stop them, but one of the
swashbucklers kicked him back down against the wall. He
groaned in pain as he grabbed his side.

Faylin awoke and whimpered, "If you see Maurna again,
tell her I'm proud of her."

"I will," the half-elf promised.

Before any more could be said, the cell door slammed and locked, leaving Saim alone. Other than the sound of the sea knocking on the hull, it was quiet, and he decided to try something he had never had in his life. He closed his eyes, lowered his head, and begged the Great Spirit for mercy.

...

Faylin felt his feet thud against every step as he was pulled up to the deck of the ship. He knew he was going to die, but even if he had the energy to fight, he had been starved, denied water, and beaten, so death sounded quite pleasant. He welcomed the idea. In fact, he prayed for it.

After he was dragged out of the stairwell, the setting sun blinded him. It wasn't that it was bright. It was because he had spent so much time hidden from it. His head pounded as he tried to focus on the silhouettes of the pirates working on the sails, but before he could, the shadow of a large bald man was cast over him.

"I take no pleasure in this," Separ grumbled, "but you had knowledge I needed."

The former king did not have any desire to stay alive, and he was not going to beg, but he had to ask, "You have the Eye of Sight Unseen, and the key to the door. Why kill me now?"

"The Eye," the captain replied, "it tells me you will try to stop me."

"How could I?" Faylin scoffed. "Besides, what if the Eye is wrong?"

"It never has been before."

"Have you ever ignored the wishes of the Eye?"

"Never wanted to."

"It's the voices of dragon's and abysmyths. What makes you think they care about a pirate warlord?"

This angered Separ, so he knelt down and grabbed the former king's face to whisper, "Because we share a common goal. I unlock the Door of Sight Unseen, and I get the treasure within. With that, I control these lands. Through me, they too have power."

"You're a fool," Faylin said, looking the Dragon's Voice in the eye. "They are using you. You haven't a clue what this treasure is, and yet you blindly follow their word."

Separ grinned and flipped his eye patch up to reveal the red orb in his socket surrounded by thick scar tissue, hissing, "Blindly? I see it all. The prize is power. And that's all I need to know. That is all I need to know."

"The prize?" wheezed the former king. "You call it a prize? What prize causes a dwarf to cut out his own tongue? Or a miserable son of a bitch to cut out his own eye and kill his own son? His son's mother? A prize doesn't come with a price this large."

"Something this sacred requires a hefty sacrifice. That which is most cherished. For this power, one that would allow me to, I would sacrifice anything. This includes you," explained Separ as he pulled the sword tucked in his belt. "Again, I take no pleasure."

A pirate placed a bucket underneath Faylin. The realization hit him that this was to catch his blood as the captain placed the blade under his chin. Finally, the pain would be over. The pain of knowing all the elves in Naughstaure he had once held dear were dead. The women. The children. The armies he'd once ruled over. They were all dead and they died believing their king betrayed them. Perhaps now he could enter the Abyss and hopefully the Great Spirit would allow him to explain that he did what he thought was right.

Suddenly, the ship quaked as if something struck the hull. A drop of blood hit the wood of the bucket as Separ's blade nicked Faylin's flesh. The captain and the pirates around the former king scanned the sea for what could have caused the disturbance.

"Did we hit something?" mumbled Separ as he quickly walked to the bridge, and shouted at the buccaneer holding the wheel. "What in the Abyss did you hit!?!"

"Nothing, sir!" replied the pirate. "Something hit us!"

The captain scowled as he walked up the steps to look out into the water, scolding the swashbuckler, "There is nothing in these seas for days, and you say something hit us!?! What could cause that kind of commotion that we couldn't see coming?"

Just then, thick tentacles, three times the size of any mast, flew out from the sea, and wrapped around the entire vessel. As the grip of the massive squid tightened, it brought the boat to a halt and tore down many of the large sails. The sudden stop caused all the pirates aboard to fall to the wooden floorboards. Separ managed to keep himself standing by grabbing one of the rails to steady himself.

The confused shouts of the crewmen halted as a massive, red, shell-covered claw gripped the other side of the deck. As it pinched down, causing the wood to collapse under its strength, another claw came up to grab the edge. This time a pirate was caught under the giant pincher, holding his torso down to the deck, and eventually it split his side open. His entrails squeezed out onto floorboards beside him, and he screamed in unbearable agony.

As the shouting of the buccaneer faded out, his life pooling around his body, the hulking crab pulled itself aboard. Separ dove down the steps leading to the bridge, barely dodging one of the massive shelled legs slamming down. On the back of the mighty crustacean rode a mage in robes made from the finest cloth and coral armor on her shoulders. The water seemed to fall around her, leaving her completely untouched by the sea, as the blue jewel atop her coral staff shined brightly.

"Surrender the half-elf!" she yelled. "Or we will pull off every board and end every life on this ship!"

...

Too weak to hold himself up, Saim fell over as he felt the ship suddenly come to a stop. He tried to lift himself off the ground, but the sound of boards creaking and snapping in the next room stopped him. After a while of glaring at the door, wondering what was happening, water began to flow out from under it.

Seawater gushed into the room, instantly turning the floor into an ankle-deep puddle. The room was filling up fast, and in only a few moments he would be submerged. He wanted to die, but not like this.

...

As the water leaked through a wide breach in the hull, a line of swashbucklers gathered, starting from the bottom of the steps and ending at a ballista window on the middle deck. The line passed a couple of buckets back and forth, filling them with water, and emptying them upstairs.

Two more pirates ran down the steps; one with wooden planks and nails in hand, the other dragging a barrel of pitch down to patch the hull. However, as they reached the hole and knelt down to begin work, two blades emerged from the source of the leak, impaling the torsos of the two buccaneers.

Havish lifted himself up from the now-thigh-deep pool, and as he pulled his coral, stone swords from the bodies, the swashbucklers left the line. As they rushed the bard, Rust popped up from the deepening sea water with dual-sided ax made from the same materials as Havish's blades.

The pirates were unprepared, and even though they were armed, they didn't have a chance against the two intruders. One swashbuckler after another fell to his end as the clattering of blades inevitably led to the deaths of more opponents. The bard and dwarf spun and slashed, and the rising water level became darker with the blood of their enemies.

…

Faylin's eyes were finally able to focus on the mage atop the colossal shelled beast, and was shocked to see who it was. He called out her name, "Maurna!"

Surprised, she pulled off the hood covering her head. Seeing the reaction of the two elves, Separ rushed to the pirates holding her king. After grabbing Faylin's neck collar, he lifted him to his feet, and placed the tip of his sword into his ribs.

"You will stop your assault," ordered the captain. "I don't think I need to say what I'm prepared to do."

"Look around you," the mage warned him. "You will not survive this."

Separ looked out into the sea, which looked empty until the army of blue-elves rose to the water's surface. Countless armed soldiers rode upon saddles connected to the backs of many humpback whales, orcas, dolphins, and sharks. Coral and stone armor covered the heads of the creatures. The ship was surrounded and outnumbered, but Separ knew he had the one thing that could keep the army at bay.

"I would sacrifice all of my men, and they would gladly lay down their lives!" the Dragon's Voice shouted. "Can you make that claim!"

Maurna scowled, knowing she could not. She had been raised by her king to believe all life was sacred, and though she still held on to prejudice against humans, she had grown over the course of her time with the travelers. She had just met the sea-elves, but she knew if they were to attack the vessel, some would never return home. This would also mean she would lose the only link she had left to her home of Naughstaure.

Separ grinned in victory as the mage was stricken silent. He had won, and all he had to do was promise not to kill just one elf. Tears fell down Faylin's face, realizing his life was the only thing in the way of the captain's defeat. And he refused to let this be a factor any longer.

Gathering every bit of strength he had left, the former king jerked his arm free of one of the pirates, grabbed hold of Separ's sword, and forced the tip of the blade deep between his own ribs. Faylin looked into the eye of the Dragon's Voice, and saw expressions he thought he would never see conveyed on his face. Shock. Disappointment. Fear.

"You will lose this, Separ," the former king choked out, his mouth filling with blood, "and seeing your torment from the Abyss will be my paradise."

Separ scowled as he pulled his sword from the dying elf, and with a smile on his face, Faylin fell limply to the ground.

"No!" Maurna shouted.

With that word, the whales closest to the ship launched blue-elves into the air with their tails and as the pirates on board got to their feet, the soldiers landed on the deck. Soon, the swashbucklers' swords clashed with the spears of the sea army, and Separ shouted orders to his crew.

"Men!" the captain cried, "battle stations!"

...

The holding cell had filled to Saim's neck. Air was becoming harder to take in. After a few more moments, his feet couldn't touch the ground as he started to float. Though he was weak, he still struggled to keep his head above the rising water. He was sure this was his end, and he could hear the men in the next room were much too busy fighting off whatever threat had made its way into the bowels of the ship.

Perhaps this was for the best. Separ couldn't open the Door of Sight Unseen without taking Saim's life at the altar, and though he wished he could see his father's defeat, he knew it wouldn't be long before he drowned. He never believed in the tales that were told of a paradise in the afterlife, but if there were such a place, he couldn't wait until he was reunited with his mother, Lurya. It would also be nice to see his horse by the same name. He wondered if Havish, Rust, and Maurna waited for him in the Abyss.

Soon, the water had filled to the ceiling, and he was in over his head. He felt weightless as he floated in the center of the holding cell. Relief. He closed his eyes and pushed his last breath from his lungs. He was at peace.

...

Rust cleaved the last buccaneer's head off his shoulders, and Havish pulled his weapons out of the flesh of his fallen opponent. The water had filled to the dwarf's shoulders, so they had even less time than they had planned to find their imprisoned ally. Panic began to set in as the bard realized the back half of the ship was already flooded.

"Saim!" he cried out.

...

Saim could see light ahead, and he walked toward it. Was this the Abyss? Was this what was described in the teachings of the Great Spirit? Was the pain of living among a world that refused to accept him finally at an end?

"Saim," said a feminine voice.

The half-elf squinted into the bright light and saw the silhouette of a woman walking toward him. As she came closer, Saim saw her pointed ears. It was an elf. No, not just an elf. It was his mother.

For so long, he couldn't remember how she looked, but there she was. Her long, light blond hair draped over her shoulders. Her light-blue eyes looked upon her son with a love and understanding that Saim only felt in long-lost memories.

She placed her hand on the half-elf's cheek, and it spread warmth throughout his body. Tears fell down Saim's face. He knew the word *happiness*, and he had often used the word to describe how he felt. But never had he realized its true meaning until this moment.

Lurya pulled him toward her, and she placed her lips on his forehead. A small kiss on his brow had never felt so sincere. She wiped the tears from his cheeks and looked into his eyes. He was home.

"Saim," she said again, but this time something was different. It sounded worried.

"Saim!" shouted a man's voice.

...

The half-elf's eyes flew open. Though the salt in the water burned them, he kept them open to see where he was. He was still floating in the holding cell of the pirate vessel.

Saim turned to the heavy door, and after swimming to it, he pounded it with his fists. The door managed to rattle despite the thick waters softening his blows. His lungs burned, he was sore and exhausted, but it didn't stop him from continuing his assault on the door. He needed to see this through. He was going to live.

...

Havish spun to look at the door next to him, which shook furiously. Rust and the bard ran to it, and began pulling on the handle, but it wouldn't budge. Havish dove under the water to see what was blocking the door from opening. A thick iron lock hung on the handle, and judging by its size, it wasn't going anywhere no matter how hard they struck it. This didn't stop the dwarf from swinging his ax into the wood, but the resistance of the water made it impossible to even make a dent in it.

It was no use. Their strength alone would not free the prisoner inside. There had to be some other way to open the door. There had to be, or else Havish would drown trying.

...

Maurna leapt off of the massive crab's back, and rushed through the sea-elves and pirates battling to the death. She managed to reach her dying king's side without catching the attention of any of her enemies along the way. She knelt down, and lifted Faylin into her lap. Though he was bleeding to death, his expression was calm as he looked into her teary eyes.

"I'm sorry," she whimpered.

"You have nothing to apologize for, my dear," he choked out. "I wanted this."

"I could have been there. I could have stopped our home from being destroyed."

"No. The Elders did this. And they paid the price for their stubborn ways. Though it was a price too harsh for anyone to have to pay, it was Separ who carried out the punishment."

"Please don't go," she begged her king. "I don't know what to do without you."

"You do," he assured. "The Dragon's Voice must be stopped. Do not let our people die in vain."

"I will stop him," she uttered as her tears landed on her king's chest.

With his last breath, he sighed to her, "I love you, Maurna."

"And I you," she said as Faylin's eyes shut, sending him to the Great Spirit's side.

She glared at his motionless face, and as she continued to stare the sound of the war around her began to become louder. She looked up, and saw that both sides of this battle had lost lives. But she had lost more than anyone would this night.

Maurna gently lay Faylin's body on the deck of the vessel, and got to her feet with a scowl. The sadness faded in her heart, and was replaced with a hate so pure, so powerful, only spilling blood could calm it.

She turned to find her victim. A lone pirate spotted her. As he ran to fight, two more joined him in his quest. The mage stood her ground, only tilting her staff toward the men with a scream. After the blue jewel lit up, a cold breeze, almost as frigid as the vengeance controlling her, blew through her hair.

Suddenly, frost covered the buccaneers, slowing their advance. Before they could even realize it, their muscles became still, and so did the blood in their veins. As if carved from a weak stone, one of the pirates fell over, breaking into a few pieces. The other two stood still. The swashbuckler leading the attack was frozen completely, but the other screamed in pain as only his body below the waist had been turned to ice.

Maurna slowly approached the frozen pirate, and once she was close enough, she used the bottom of her staff to smash his head into several jagged segments. The other watched in horror, but was only able to shiver in panic as she turned to him. She was close enough for the man to see the tears rolling down her cheeks, which were illuminated by the red glow from the jewel atop her staff. Only more pain went through the buccaneer's legs as they defrosted, but before he could fall to his knees, he was lit aflame.

His sword fell to her feet as she watched him burn, and she knelt down to pick it up. It was hot enough to instantly blister the palm of her hand, but she didn't dare drop it. Not until she could feel a warm splash of blood on her knuckles from one of the many living men still alive around her.

...

Havish looked around in the room for anything that could break the lock on the thick door as Rust continued to fight the force of the water to swing his ax. He knew he had very little time, because the door had ceased in movement. In the bard's panic, he spotted a couple of spare anchors leaning against the wall by the steps, and a small length of rope hanging on a hook.

"Help me," Havish cried, splashing through the sea water to the anchor.

The dwarf ran to his side, and assisted the bard in dragging the heavy iron to the large hole in the side of the ship. Havish took the rope, and quickly tied a thick knot around the ring atop the anchor. Then after splashing in the water back to the door, he dove under. The seawater stung his eyes as he forced them open to see himself tying the rope to the lock.

He popped back out from under the water, and ordered Rust to, "Throw the anchor out."

With all his might, he pushed the heavy iron out of the hole in the ship. The anchor sunk quickly into the sea, until it suddenly pulled the rope taut. For a moment, it seemed like Havish's plan wasn't going to work, until the sound of creaking wood could be heard.

"Step back," the bard commanded.

Just as Rust and Havish stepped away from door and the breach in the hull, the lock pulled a plank away from the door. The rope whipped into the ceiling of the ship, cracking the wood with the lock, then it followed the anchor to the bottom of the sea.

The bard pulled the door open, and instantly spotted Saim floating motionless in the water. He quickly pulled the unconscious half-elf out of the holding cell. With Rust's help, he pulled Saim over to the steps, away from the water, then put his ear to the half-elf's mouth. Havish had never felt a breath so rewarding against his cheek until then.

"He's all right," the bard cheered.

"Good," said Rust with a smile. "Let's get him out of here."

With that, Havish and the dwarf brought Saim to the hole in the ship, and dove into the water.

...

The ship's ballista bolts fell into the water, killing a few of the sea-elves and their whale, but the swashbucklers' lives were dwindling. The dragon stables had finally been opened, and the winged beasts took flight with men on their backs. As they flew out over the sea, one was instantly rammed out of the sky by a whale leaping out of the water. Before the beast could return to the air, it was torn apart by sharks.

Far out in the water, a sea-elf general standing atop a massive sea turtle gave the signal for the rangers armed with crossbows to fire among the oncoming dragons. The winged beasts attempted to dodge all the bolts, but there were far too many. Some managed to escape the projectiles, but the rest were wounded. Another fell from the sky, providing a meal for the bloodthirsty fish below.

Out of the corner of the general's eye, he saw Havish and Rust pull the unconscious Saim onto one of the large turtles' shells. The bard nodded to the sea-elf signaling their victory, so the general shouted the elven order to retreat. This started a wave of voices calling out the same command to alert the rest of their army.

Soon, the soldiers mounted on the whales, sharks, and dolphins turned from the broken pirate ship, and quickly dove under water. The giant squid let go of the vessel, sinking below, and the behemoth crustacean stopped slamming its heavy claws down onto random swashbucklers to crawl back into the sea.

Morst, still casting flames onto some the few buccaneers left on the ship, halted his attack as he saw his fellow warriors diving overboard, and heard the call to retreat. He looked out at the rangers in the distance, who were dipping the heads of their crossbow bolts into buckets of the sticky flammable liquid in front of them. Just as he was about to follow his army back out to sea, he turned to see Maurna still slashing away at the enemy, unaware of what was happening.

He ran to her side, calling her name, "Maurna."

She spun to face Morst with the jewel of her staff glowing in his face. Once she realized it was him, the jewel faded.

"What!?!" she screamed angrily.

"We're leaving!" he replied.

"No!" she shouted. "Not until every man on this ship is dead!"

Morst walked closer, placing his hand on the blade she had taken grumbling, "The mission was not to kill them. It was to save your ally."

The hate faded from her face as she asked, "We have him?"

"Aye."

A small smile crossed her face, but faded as blood splashed on her. Morst looked down at his chest, where the crimson tip of a blade stuck out. He gurgled on the blood rushing into his throat, and fell limply onto the floor, revealing Separ pulling his sword from the sea-elf's back.

Before he could swing his weapon toward Maurna, she slammed her staff on the bridge to conjure a wind so strong, the captain stumbled backward. Then he was thrown into the empty dragon stables, smashing one of the wooden doors.

Maurna looked down at Morst, who was only conscious enough to whisper, "Go."

With a nod, she ran to the edge of the boat and leapt into the sea just as a barrage of flaming crossbow bolts stuck into the top of the boat. If the general mage were not already dead, the several hot projectiles piercing his flesh would have done it. The remaining pirates on the deck were struck down by the bolts, and one managed to bury itself into Separ's thigh.

Maurna began to tire out from swimming toward the rangers, and she wasn't sure how much longer she could go. Just before she could give up, a dolphin instantly dove between her legs, and carried her to safety.

Saim began to come to as he heard crossbows firing, so he gasped and sat up, thinking he was under attack. When he saw the sinking pirate ship going down in the distance, he realized it was the exact opposite. Havish and Rust greeted him with laughter as they shook him excitedly.

"Welcome back!" the dwarf shouted with glee.

The half-elf wanted to reply, but he was still in agony from the beating he had taken. Through his wincing, he saw Maurna riding up on the dolphin, and could only smile through the pain.

The bard helped her atop the turtle's shell, and she instantly ran to Saim. She wrapped her arms around his neck, and he responded in kind. He felt warm, much like he did when his mother held him. That's when he realized this warmth had a word to describe it. Love.

Back on the ship, Separ howled in pain from the bolt embedded in his leg as he looked at his flaming, sinking vessel, and the few dragons circling the ship with nowhere to land. All was quiet but the crackle of the flames spreading, and the tattered sails on his mast flapping in the wind.

He snapped the bolt off inside his thigh with a scream, got to his feet, and limped to the wheel of his ship. As he looked out onto the several dead bodies of his crew, he realized for the first time in a long time, he had lost.

Chapter XIX

The night sky twinkled with thousands of stars as the sea-elves dropped the travelers off at the shoreline of the Southern Continent. They let them keep the weapons and armor they had borrowed, and gave Saim one of their crossbows with plenty of bolts in a quiver.

Havish would have asked them for more help, but they had already done so much without asking for anything in return. They even transported their mounts to the coast.

Vawn had told his people to get the travelers enough supplies and food to last a few days, but seeing as how they were still elves, regardless of their underwater home, they could only offer kelp and dried seaweed for sustenance.

Rust usually turned away anything without meat, but it was a necessity, and he thought it best not to add to the tension he had felt since he told them of his treachery. Even though it was before he'd begun this journey with them, he had still caused quite a bit of grief because of it, though Porter had no issues turning up his snout to the tasteless food.

The fact they were now on a giant desert meant that dried wood was easy to come by. In fact, before the large turtles that left them on the coast were out of sight, the travelers had collected enough firewood to last them until morning.

According to stories about this land the bard had heard, the nights were rather cold, so the campfire would be essential. The sea-elves didn't have access to flint to ignite a flame, so it was very fortunate they had a mage with them.

Once again, they had to shed most of their clothing to dry next to the fire. This made staying warm a bit more difficult, but with the wet clothing they were sure to catch their death.

The dwarf and his boar sat close together, as did Havish and his horse. Saim leaned against Lurya with Maurna next to him, but they were at a distance from the bard and dwarf so they could speak privately. However, they couldn't seem to find words to say. Silence overcame them as they listened to the water splash along the beach, and the fire crackling.

Finally, Saim whispered, "I'm sorry."

"Why?" asked Maurna.

"Faylin," he said weakly. "I couldn't save him."

"Nor could I," she sighed. "He went bravely."

"That he did. When they took him from the cell we shared, he didn't beg for his life. He only wanted me to tell you something. He's proud of you."

The mage didn't know what to say. She had always known this, because he had said it before, but knowing this was the last time he would began to stir up the sadness inside her again.

Before a tear could touch her cheek, Saim quickly wiped it away. And as if by instinct, he brought her face to his chest. It was what his mother would do when he would cry as a child. No matter how small or large the reason, whether it was accidentally falling down or having just dealt with one of Separ's interrogations, it always warranted her to console him the same way.

Saim didn't expect Maurna to take to it the way he did so long ago, but he was wrong. She leaned against him and held his hand in her lap.

Warmth flowed through his body, but it didn't make him as happy as it had before. Instead, he felt her sorrow. Maybe this was what love did to people, giving one the choice to feel the emotions of another, and choosing to do so even if the feeling was unpleasant. The only thing he felt, that he was sure she didn't, was curiosity.

He wondered if she too felt that warmth and connection. In truth, she did feel it, and she also wondered if he did as well. They shared more than they realized.

Havish watched the half-elf comfort the mage, and it reminded him of when he was a young bard. The young women would swoon from his stories and the songs he would play on his flute.

Rust peered at the smile on the human's face as he stared at Saim and Maurna and said, "Young love, eh? Between an abomination and an elf nonetheless."

"Maybe the boy prefers elves," laughed Havish. "I guess it's the one thing the boy got from his father."

Rust chuckled as he stared at the campfire.

After some silence, the bard said, "I don't blame you for what happened."

"You don't?"

"Separ was going to find us regardless of speaking to you. It was only a matter of time."

"Maybe," grumbled the dwarf. "But I certainly didn't help things."

"Saim is safe, and he wouldn't be without your aid," Havish uttered as he met Rust's eyes. "You have proven your loyalty, and I forgive you."

The dwarf smiled, and after some quiet, he joked, "So after this, I'm still getting paid?"

As the bard gave a confused look to Rust, he saw the grin on his face. Then they both shared a hearty laugh.

Perhaps the reason the travelers felt it necessary to relax with some conversation was because it would only be a short trip to the caves, which led to the Door of Sight Unseen. Stories didn't warn of the dangers inside, but this could very well mean no man had survived to tell them. It was a possibility the travelers may not live through the next night. On top of that, they were to seal a mystical door, and they had no idea how they were going to do it. They only knew it had to be done.

Despite knowing they may be marching to their end the next day, they slept soundly. It was the most restful night they'd had since starting this endeavor. Maybe it was because they knew they were soon to the end, and even though it could be tragic, it would still be over. This was somehow a relief.

As the sun began to rise, Saim and Maurna woke up in each other's arms, leaning against Lurya. Havish arose beside his horse, and Rust sat up from leaning on Porter all night. After a quick stretch and a light meal of kelp, they packed their gear onto their mounts and got on their way.

The mage and the half-elf shared a ride on Lurya's back, which made the heat no less bearable as the bright ball of light in the sky shined down on their shoulders. Every now and again, desert creatures could be seen hunting for sustenance in groups. Other than that, there wasn't another soul around as far as the eye could see. Though their sight was untrustworthy due to the hot waves caused by the sun beating down on the scorching sand.

This land was unforgiving. Maurna would often use her staff to search for any hidden sources of water, but there was none to be found other than what was given to them by the sea-elves. It was difficult to ration it, but the travelers had to do so, or else risk dehydration in the sweltering weather. Any care-lessness of their supplies would surely end up in death before they reached their destination, which seemed so far away. Any progression they made atop their mounts seemed to be meaning-less, because only more sand and rocks could be seen ahead.

The Southern Continent wasn't always this desolate. There was once more settlements in the Southern Continent than any other. Cities where elves and humans lived in peace, but this had been before the war. The two sides had nearly wiped each other out, and when the trade routes were abandoned, everyone moved to the coast. Soon the cargo ships became a part of the bloodshed. Once supplies stopped coming, both the elves and humans had no choice but to leave their home forever. Only the bones of those lost in battle remained. A few stuck out of the sand, but the countless others were buried deep from the many sandstorms that had blown through since then.

After a long while of travel, the sun was about to touch the horizon. This meant the heat wouldn't be a factor much longer, but it had already taken its toll on the bard. Rust, Saim, and Maurna had almost forgotten their bodies were more attuned to high temperatures, so it was quite a surprise when Havish fell off his horse, kicking up a cloud of dust from the ground.

After climbing off of their mounts, the dwarf, half-elf, and mage ran to the human's side. His eyes were fighting to stay open, his skin was red, he had stopped sweating, and his lips were splitting from blistering dryness. Rust instantly pulled out his canteen and poured it in the bard's mouth. He choked on it for a moment, but eventually began taking big gulps.

"He's overheated," the dwarf declared before turning to Havish. "Take what you must, but leave a bit for my boar."

The human finished drinking, and with Saim's help, he sat up to whisper, "I'm not going to last out here much longer. Leave me. Get to the Door."

"We're not leaving you," Maurna assured him.

"I will only slow your travels," insisted the bard. "My life means nothing if we do not close the Door of Sight Unseen."

"You never left me," Saim groaned as he lifted Havish to a standing position. "Now, let's go."

He helped the human onto his horse and climbed on behind him to make sure Havish stayed awake. Meanwhile, Rust and the mage climbed on Porter and Lurya.

They continued on, but picked up the pace. Before the bard was completely cooked, they had to find shade, but the only place they knew to have shade was their destination at the caves. With Maurna being finely attuned to the land, they made haste with her lead.

With the sun sinking halfway down the sky, they had finally seen a tall mountain coming closer. There were tall rocks and plateaus along the way, but this was the only mountain in the entire desert. It had to be what they were looking for, and as they got closer they became much more positive.

A large opening in the side of the mountain had dwarven bones strewn about the ground outside; and ominous words, in both human and elven language, lined the rim of the tunnel opening, and offered warning of abysmyths inside. Everyone hoped the ancient signs meant the warnings didn't apply any longer, but it was wishful thinking.

Havish moaned as he almost fell over again, but Saim propped him back up, and headed inside. The half-elf was scared of the dangers within the cave, but he was much more terrified of losing the bard. With a bit of reluctance, Rust and Maurna followed Saim into the tunnel.

Once inside, the half-elf climbed off the horse, assisted Havish in getting down, and helped the bard sit against the wall.

"We'll rest here for a while," said Saim. "At least until the sun goes down."

"I'll be fine," Havish grumbled. "Just go. Close the Door."

"No," the half-elf uttered. "We've plenty of time, and we'll need your help."

Without the threat of Separ, there was no rush to close the Door of Sight Unseen, so despite the bard's protest, they were not going anywhere.

While Saim tended to Havish, Rust and Maurna walked around the massive cavern to make sure they were alone. The tunnels were vast and deep, but considering dragons once roamed this place to fight off the abysmyths, it needed to be this size.

The dwarf pointed out the jewels and metal ore shining in the dim light coming in from the cave opening. This would bring wealth beyond his wildest dreams, but instead, he settled for the unlit torch held in a sconce on the wall.

After taking the torch, he walked to the mage and asked her, "Can I trouble you for some fire?"

"Of course," she replied with a smirk.

She touched the jewel of her staff to the torch, and once it began to glow red, the wood lit aflame. As the flame brightened the area around Rust and Maurna, they saw the rocky face of an abysmyth next to them.

They both gasped, readied their weapons, and Porter instantly rushed to protect his owner. But after a moment, they all sighed with relief, realizing that the abysmyth wasn't moving.

Its body didn't have the glow of lava flowing through its veins. Instead, the molten rock had leaked onto the ground around it and hardened, holding in place the hammer buried in its chest.

"At least we know we can kill one by ourselves," mumbled the mage.

"Aye," agreed Rust. "I suppose that's comforting."

Meanwhile, Saim gave Havish a sip from his canteen. The bard pulled his lips away and leaned his head against the wall with a sigh. After looking into the half-elf's eyes, he reached up and grabbed his shoulder as if to show his gratitude.

"When you were a child," the bard began, "I cut your ears, because I didn't want anyone to harm you for being part elf."

"I know," Saim said.

"I never forgave myself for it. When you ran away, I thought you'd be safer. From Separ and me."

"I can only imagine the burden you endured while taking care of a child that wasn't even yours. I didn't understand when I was young, but I realize now that I wouldn't have been safe if it weren't for you."

Havish smiled, but before he could respond, a screech was heard from outside the cave, and the ground rumbled as if something heavy had landed nearby. Rust and Maurna spun to face the opening, but nothing could be seen.

"Dragons," the dwarf uttered.

"How?" pondered the mage aloud. "We burned Separ's ship and all of his supplies with it."

"But we didn't kill him," Rust mumbled.

"You have to leave me, Saim," ordered the bard with panic in his eyes. "They're coming."

"No," the half-elf replied. "We can fight them."

Havish used the stone wall to clumsily get to his feet, and after pulling his swords, he growled, "I'll hold them off."

"Alone?" scoffed Saim. "You won't stand a chance."

"He won't be alone," announced the dwarf as he and Porter stood by the bard's side.

After giving Rust a nod of thanks, Havish turned back to the half-elf to give the orders, "Take the horses. Get to the Door. Close it."

"But—"

"There is no discussion, boy," the bard interrupted. "Go! Now!"

With a grunt, Saim ran to Maurna and helped her onto Havish's steed. Then after mounting Lurya, he turned back to the bard, dwarf, and boar.

"Be safe," he uttered.

Porter assured him with a grunt, while the bard just said, "You as well."

With that, the half-elf rode away with the mage right behind him. Everything in Saim's body told him to turn around and fight, but he knew the Door had to be closed. And Maurna was the only one who could figure out how to do it. He had to protect her. He needed to. He must.

Havish, Rust, and Porter watched Saim and the mage ride further into the cave, then spun to face the heavy footsteps coming their way from the opening. They knew this could be the end of the road for them, but so be it. Whatever was coming may strike them down, but the bard, dwarf, and boar would certainly make it a difficult victory to claim.

Chapter XX

Saim and Maurna rode their horses with haste through the tremendous cave, dodging stalagmites and ducking under stalactites as they followed the tunnel. The hooves of the steeds echoed all through the caverns, which twisted and turned. Sweat collected on each of their brows from the climbing temperature as they traveled lower into the mountain and only the light atop the mage's staff lit the way.

"What do we do when we find it?" shouted the half-elf over the stomping of their steeds.

"Maybe we collapse the cave!" Maurna replied.

"But couldn't the abysmyths still get through it?"

"I haven't seen any."

Just as she finished her sentence, the smell of sulfur entered their nostrils, and after a distant growl, they slowed their horses to a walk. After rounding a corner, they saw the source of the smell and sound.

Farther down the tunnel, a red glow could be seen. A glow that looked like several cracks in the rock. But they were moving. And they weren't all moving together as one. It was the hot molten rock flowing through the veins of the beasts made of stone. Monsters from the Abyss. At least six of them.

"There they are," whispered Saim.

The half-elf watched in horror, realizing this was the only way to go. Retreat wasn't an option. There was only forward.

"Let's go," Maurna commanded as she nudged the side of Havish's horse with her foot.

The horse darted forward, and Saim followed atop Lurya's back. Instantly, the abysmyths heard them approaching and let out a deafening shriek. The mage's jaw dropped and she cried out to let the creatures know she feared them not.

As the steeds and abysmyths charged at each other, the half-elf pulled the crossbow from his back, and quickly loaded a bolt from his quiver.

...

The rumbling of the dragon's footsteps came closer, and the beating of Havish's heart seemed to drown it out in his ears. His already weakened body quivered at the thoughts of his mortality, and the secrets he wished he would have admitted to that would die with him. To Rust, this fight meant he could redeem his existence of selfishness and deceit. Porter, on the other hand, only wanted to protect the dwarf that looked over him for so long. They each had their reasons to be victorious, but victory had to be the result, no matter what.

The clawed, scaled feet of the beast finally came down in view of the dwarf and bard, and the massive wingspan blocked the view of the dim light coming through the opening. They both squinted at the silhouette of the monster, and realized there was more to this threat. Something on its back.

As Rust threw his torch forward to shed light on the oncoming danger, they saw every detail of the black, horned dragon and the man on its back. The captain of the now-destroyed pirate ship. The Dragon's Voice. Separ.

"There you are," he began. "I'd hoped to see you here."

"You will not go any farther," grumbled Rust.

"Is that right?" the captain asked as the sound of more footsteps rumbled behind him.

The rumbling became louder as two more dragons landed in the entrance of the cave. The light was completely blocked out, and the dwarf and bard were outnumbered. It was hopeless, but victory must still be had.

"You should have killed me like you did the rest of my crew," said Separ in a laugh.

"It was a mistake," Havish replied, "one we shall not make again."

"Indeed," mumbled the captain as the dragon he was upon raised its head to inhale deeply.

Rust and the bard dove in opposite directions, letting exhaled fire blow between them, and Porter hurried to flank the attackers. The dwarf instantly charged Separ's dragon, but it turned slightly to whip him with its tail. This sent Rust flying through the air, and into the corpse of the abysmyth deeper inside the cave. It crumbled apart, as the dwarf stumbled back to his feet with a groan.

One of the other two monsters jumped toward Havish, but his reflexes were too dulled for him to move out of the way in time. Luckily, Porter knew this, and rushed under the dragon, digging his tusks into the beast's soft belly. After pushing the monster away, the boar nudged the bard away from the dragon's reach.

Once Havish regained his footing, he noticed the third dragon scaling the wall to the ceiling. As it crawled along the top of the cave over the bard, it looked down at him to blow down a storm of flame. Havish tried to move away, but he was still much too weak, and only fell backward. He brought his arms in front of his face as if to futilely block the fire that would surely burn him to death.

Just as the flame escaped the monster's lips, it was struck in its scaly, horned face by the stone head of the long-dead abysmyth thrown by Rust. The flames shot along the ground and walls as the beast fell off the ceiling, toward the fallen bard.

Havish quickly rolled to dodge the bone-crushing weight of the creature headed toward him, but from where the dwarf saw, he didn't appear to roll far enough. The rumble of the dragon's body hitting the ground shook the whole cave, and the bard was out of sight.

Suddenly, the monster howled in pain as a hand holding a blade came down into its side. Then another blade was stabbed into him, as Havish used his swords to lift himself onto the creature, stabbing it deep as he climbed upon its torso. As he stood on the dragon's midsection, the beast attempted to bite him, but he only thrust his blade through the soft roof of its mouth. The monster went limp, pulling the sword from the bard's grasp.

Meanwhile, Porter was still dealing with his own winged opponent. As it recoiled from the fresh wounds in its stomach, it swiped at the boar with its claws. Porter ducked under the beast's attack, and again lunged with his tusks forward.

However, the dragon was much too quick, and used its wings to lift itself into the air. After landing behind the boar, it quickly bit down into Porter's back. The boar squealed in agony as the creature shook its head, ripping the flesh from his bones.

"No!" Rust screamed while running to the aid of his best friend.

The dragon released Porter to turn toward the shouting dwarf, but as it tried to spray fire upon him, Rust dropped to his back and slid under the beast. As he skidded below the monster, he sunk the blade of his ax into its abdomen. Continuing to slide out from under the dragon, its entrails spilled onto the stone floor behind the dwarf. The creature fell lifeless with a screech, but as Rust got back to his feet, he noticed that Porter too had fallen.

Separ ordered his mount to torch Havish, who still remained on the corpse of the fallen creature. As the fire rained down, the bard darted under the wing of the corpse. The flames poured around him, and the heat was so intense, his hand holding the massive wing in front of him began to burn, though he didn't dare move, or the rest of his body would suffer.

...

Maurna raced toward the abysmyth, holding her staff up high, and Saim followed with his crossbow ready to fire. As the horses carried them closer, the jewel on her staff began to glow brighter. Just as the first abysmyth raised its clawed hand to strike, the mage swung her staff down.

Suddenly, the cave ceiling broke into large boulders, crushing the monster underneath. Havish's horse jumped over the rubble, and continued toward the next beast. This time she raised her staff, and the ground beneath the abysmyth forced it into the top of the tunnel so hard it broke off its arm. Lava poured down the stones as Saim ducked under the falling massive stone limb, barely missing the half-elf and slamming on rocks behind him.

The third creature was pressed against the wall as a stone pillar grew from the side of the cave. Its molten blood sprayed across Maurna's path, and she was headed right for it. She pulled back on the horse's reins to slow it, but it panicked. It reared back with a startled neigh, throwing her to the ground. Then it ran into two of the three monsters still standing, and they instantly picked the steed up with their claws. The horse cried out in pain as the abysmyths' touch burned its flesh, but the screams were silenced as it was quickly pulled apart.

The sight of one of her kind being reduced to an unrecognizable bloody mess struck fear into Lurya, who immediately stopped running and started pacing behind the river of lava pouring from the crushed monster. Then the abysmyths turned their attention from the slaughtered horse to the elf using her staff to get back on her feet.

Maurna's eyes darted to the colossal stalactites above the beasts' heads, and she rapped on the ground with the bottom of her coral rod. The ground rumbled and small pebbles fell from the ceiling, bouncing off the abysmyths' heads. As they raised their hands, which hissed with blood sizzling on their claws, the mage covered her head.

Suddenly, the sharp stones above cracked and fell, impaling the monsters with a barrage of rock spears. Lava flowed from the creatures' wounds and began pooling on the ground. Maurna was surrounded by molten rock, and it was closing in around her.

Saim gave Lurya's side a slight kick, and she ran as fast as she could toward the spreading burning liquid. Then the horse leapt with all her power over the swelling pool as the half-elf reached out to Maurna. While in the air, he managed to grab her hand and lift her off the ground, just as one of the abysmyths slid down the stone that impaled it, and splashed into the lava.

After landing on the other side and avoiding the bright orange fluid, Saim, the mage, and Lurya tumbled on the hard ground. The horse stumbled to stand, but one of her legs was clearly injured as she limped back to her rider. Lurya whimpered in pain, and was much too dazed to notice the last monster stomping up behind her.

The half-elf quickly rolled onto his heels and fired his crossbow at the beast's head. But it only glanced off its hardened flesh. It wasn't hurt, but it got its attention.

Maurna had dropped her staff during the rescue, and as she glanced around to locate it, she saw it become swallowed in the magma behind them. Her only means of defense was gone.

"No," the mage whispered.

With a scowl on his face, Saim quickly reloaded his weapon and raised it to his shoulder. He stared down the bolt into the red sockets of the abysmyth and took a deep breath. The monster lowered its jaw to release an ear-piercing shriek, but the half-elf did not flinch while the ground shook with the voice of the beast. He didn't even blink as the sweat dripping from his brow began to burn his eyes. On his slow exhale, he pulled the trigger.

The whip of his crossbow sounded, followed by the whistle of the projectile ripping through the wind. Then with a thud, the bolt stopped inside the abysmyth's eye. It screamed in agony, stumbling backward and tried to pull the bolt from its head. As lava poured from the wound, the bolt dissolved to only increase the flow of the creature's life source.

Finally, the monster fell to its knees, and after a moan, it slumped over onto the wall of the cave. That was where it stayed. That was where it died.

Lurya continued to limp to Saim and nuzzled her nose against his face. After patting his horse on the neck, the half-elf turned to help up the mage who was frozen in desperation. She stared at the molten rock crawling on the ground with tears in her eyes, but no expression on her face.

"Are you all right?" he asked, lifting her to her feet.

"No," she replied. "My staff. It's gone."

Saim turned her gaze to him with his hand, and whispered, "Are *you* all right?"

"Yes."

"Then let's go," he commanded, leading her farther down the tunnel, "Lurya's hurt. We'll have to go on foot."

Maurna nodded, and followed the half-elf to the orange glow coming from deeper in the mountain. The horse tried to keep up, but the injury to her leg was too severe, so Saim and the mage slowed their pace.

Most would have put down an injured animal if it could no longer serve its purpose, but Maurna loved all living things, and the half-elf owed the steed his life. Besides, Saim had already lost one Lurya and didn't want to lose another.

...

Realizing that two dragons had already died, the captain leapt off his beast, and ordered it to deal with the dwarf. Just as he landed on the dead monster Havish was using to shield from the fire, Separ grimaced as the pain shot through his wounded leg. While holding the half of the crossbow bolt still in his thigh, the captain pulled the sword from his belt. A quick slash across the dead creature's wing revealed the bard underneath. Reaching through the cut in the wing, the captain wrapped his hand around Havish's neck, and pulled him through it.

Rust knelt down beside Porter, who was shivering from the painful and deep wounds in his back. Tears welled in the dwarf's eyes as he realized the warm and wet liquid under his knees was the blood pooling around his boar. He had failed his best friend.

Porter was not much longer for this world, but he still tried to nudge Rust out of the way of the black dragon reaching for him. It was too late. The beast wrapped its clawed hand around the dwarf's body, and lifted him off his feet. Rust swung his ax at the monster's face, but it jerked its head away, and slammed the dwarf hard on the stone floor.

All the air in Rust's lungs was forced out as he felt a couple of his ribs snap. The dragon picked up the dwarf, who was fighting to stay awake through the pain. Soon, Rust was unable to hold onto his ax any longer, so he let it go. All the sound began to muffle in his ears, and he could barely hear his ax clang on the ground.

Separ sneered in Havish's face, as the bard glared in horror at the creature holding up Rust's weakened body. The captain put his blade against the bard's cheek, forcing him to look into his eyes. Havish tried to raise his sword, but his arm was trapped on the other side of the torn wing.

"Where is Saim?" Separ growled.

"You're too late," Havish hissed from his squeezed throat. "He is closing the Door. You've lost."

"He cannot close the Door," the captain laughed as he tapped on the jewel in his eye socket with the tip of his sword. "Not without this."

Knowing he was beaten, the bard spit in Separ's face. After a scowl, the Dragon's Voice brought down his forehead into the bridge of Havish's nose. Dazed, the bard fell backward to the stone floor, and after hopping off the dead dragon's body,

Separ knocked Havish unconscious with a blow from the handle of his blade.

As the captain turned to his beast, he gave the order, "Let's go."

The monster threw Rust against the wall, and knelt down to let Separ on its back. Once mounted, the dragon picked up the unconscious bard gently in its mouth. The captain wanted Havish alive. He was the perfect bait to catch a half-elf.

The broken dwarf watched the Dragon's Voice ride his beast farther into the cave with the captive bard, but he was having difficulty focusing with the darkness closing in on his vision. Rust had trouble taking in a breath as he looked to Porter, who was using his last bit of life to crawl to the dwarf. The boar rested his face on Rust's lap, and looked into his eyes.

Tears fell into his red beard, as he pet the snout on the dying boar. Porter fought to keep his eyes open, but they became much too heavy. He blinked once. Then again. But on the third time of his eyes closing they didn't open again, and the dwarf felt Porter's last breath.

"To the Abyss, friend," whimpered Rust. "I will see you soon."

With that, Rust too closed his eyes.

Chapter XXI

Saim and Maurna had finally reached the center of the mountain. As they walked through the entrance of the room, they were overwhelmed by a wave of sweltering heat. A long rocky bridge hung over the bubbling lava far below and led to a platform on the other side. On the platform was an altar in front of a stone door with a dragon's head carved in it, and it was lit by a flowing stream of magma cascading down the walls on each side.

"The Door," whispered the mage. "I never thought I would see it."

The half-elf was taken aback by it as well, but he knew he had to hurry. Even if Havish, Rust, and Porter managed to hold off the dragon at the entrance, more would surely be on the way. Maurna reached for his hand, and he for hers.

Before taking the first step onto the stone bridge, Saim turned to Lurya and gave the order, "Stay here."

The horse snorted to let the half-elf know she understood.

Though the walkway was sturdy, being able to see the lava far below put knots in Saim's stomach. With each step, a few small pebbles broke off from the edge of the bridge, and the half-elf watched them fall for what seemed like hours before hitting the molten rock.

"Don't look down," he warned.

Maurna kept her eyes forward, looking at the dragon's face in the Door ahead as the heat caused waves in her vision. She only looked down at her feet when the room began to rumble for a few moments.

Saim pulled her close to ensure she didn't lose her balance. Allowing Separ to open the Door of Sight Unseen would be a travesty, but losing Maurna would be worse.

Once the rumbling ended, they continued to advance down the stone bridge. It was only a short walk, but the elevated height made it seem much farther.

When they finally reached the other side, the heat from the magma falls instantly began to burn their eyes. Squinting through the scalding air, they approached the altar.

"What do we do?" the mage asked.

"Perhaps you could flood this place with the lava below," Saim replied.

It would have been an excellent idea, until Maurna reminded the half-elf, "How? My staff is gone."

Saim mumbled a number of curses under his breath, keeping his eyes locked on the stone dragon on the Door. He sighed and placed his hands on the altar, but before he could wonder how to permanently shut the Door, the rumbling began again.

The mage and half-elf looked around nervously as they heard the lava below begin to bubble. They both peered over the edge of the platform into the glowing red lake below, and gasped at the cause of the commotion.

Large boulders slowly rose from the magma, but after the lava ran off, it was clear it wasn't just stone. Arms sprouted from the rocks with long sharp talons at their ends. Abysmyths. More than Saim and Maurna could count. More than they wanted to.

The creatures looked upward at Saim and Maurna and let out a scream. Once the monsters lowered their heads, they splashed through the lava to the walls of the volcano. The beasts dug their claws deep into the rock and lifted themselves out of the magma. The glowing crimson liquid dripped off of the abysmyths as they climbed farther up.

"They're coming!" shouted the mage just before asking the Great Spirit for help in her tongue.

As the monsters got closer, Maurna's prayers became louder and faster. Panic began to set in as the half-elf realized the Door had to be shut now, but he had no idea how to do it. He searched his memory for any kind of hint that might help him, but he drew only a blank.

Why would Faylin send them on this futile quest? It never made any sense to Saim, but now he wondered why he hadn't protested this. Why had he gone along with it? Why had everyone else? A sense of duty? Faith?

All the half-elf could be sure of was that his own faith was weakening. His fellow travelers were fighting to buy him enough time to do something he had no clue how to do. They were all going to die because they foolishly believed they could claim victory with ignorance.

Suddenly, Saim's thoughts were interrupted by the heavy footsteps of something entering the room. Lurya began to neigh nervously at the opening in the room. But she was quickly silenced as a clawed hand grabbed her from the shadows and pulled her out of the light. A short whine echoed just before a loud thud shook the ground. Blood instantly ran out of the tunnel.

Sadness flooded the half-elf's heart. So much, he could hardly stand. He whimpered as he clumsily took a step forward and fought to take in a breath. The tears welling in his eyes began to impair his vision as he lifted his crossbow.

"Lurya!" Saim cried out, aiming at the darkness.

As the beast came into the illumination of the lava, the half-elf and mage realized how much worse the situation had become. Havish hung limply in the mouth of the black dragon, and Separ sat grinning upon its back.

"Throw your weapon and quiver below," ordered the captain, "or I tell my dragon to bite down."

Rust and Porter were nowhere to be seen, so that could only mean one thing. They were lost. The bard was motionless, so he may have been lost as well, but in case he wasn't, Saim thought it best to comply.

Soon his crossbow and bolts were falling down into the lava and out of sight. Maurna and the half-elf were not out-numbered, but they were unarmed. Thus, they were outmatch-ed. There was no doubt in their minds that they would meet the fate of the rest of their group.

"You honestly thought you could stop this?" the pirate captain shouted over the rumbling of the molten rock and the growls of the approaching hoard of abysmyths. "This treasure has always been mine, for the Eye of Sight Unseen is in my pos-session."

"Damn you!" cried Saim. "Why is it so important? You made the promise to my mother to rule the world with her, and you killed her! Now you would kill your only son? You may rule the world, but you will be alone!"

Separ jumped off his beast's back, and landed on his feet with a wince. "I have my dragon. And more are on the way. They've done more for me than any other being. They have proven more useful than any soldier I have commanded."

"Look around you!" Maurna screamed. "We are surrounded by abysmyths. We will all die here."

"Of course we are surrounded," replied the captain as he motioned to the monsters climbing the walls. "The abysmyths are the guards of the Abyss and the Door of Sight Unseen, but to keep them underground, the Great Spirit created dragons. This is why the Eye is needed to open this Door."

Separ turned to his scaly mount and nodded. With that, the beast dropped Havish's motionless body onto the ground and took flight. The abysmyths swung their arms, attempting to swat at the winged creature, but it managed to dodge the claws and pull one off the wall, sending it back into the lake of molten rock. Without hesitation the dragon went on to attack the rest of the monsters.

The captain picked up the bard by his collar and began to drag him across the bridge. After reaching the middle of the bridge, Separ stopped, and held Havish over the lava boiling below.

"You have lost, son," announced Separ as he pulled his sword from his belt. "Believe it or not, I take no pleasure in this, but sacrifice is necessary for the greater good."

He threw his sword across the bridge at Saim's feet. The half-elf glared at the blade for a while before picking it up. With weapon in hand he took a step toward the bridge.

"Don't be foolish, boy!" the captain said as he held the bard out farther over the magma. "Complete your destiny, and I will spare the lives of your friends. Fight, and they die."

Saim froze, and as he thought out his options, Maurna grabbed his shoulder.

"Don't do this," she pleaded. "He can't be trusted."

"I am a man of my word," Separ corrected her. "Look at this world. Look at how the elves, dwarves, and humans refused to help you. They knew they were doomed, and yet they were too cowardly, proud, and bigoted to save their own lives. With this power, I will be king of all. I will be fair. Just. Can any other king say that with honesty?"

"You are a murderer!" shouted Maurna.

"Think of how many have fallen, so someone could take power," explained the Dragon's Voice. "Like all leaders, blood is on my hands. The only difference is that I did it. I didn't send men to die without taking on the same burdens myself. Can any other king say that?"

"Don't listen to him," the mage whispered in the half-elf's deformed ear.

Separ lowered his voice and met eyes with his sacrifice to say, "Saim. I promise you. This world will be better off. I will bring peace. I will end the bigotry you experienced your entire life. The prejudice that made you scar yourself. You will be the savior to the continents. I will be their leader, but you will be their deity. Even mine."

The half-elf lowered the sword and looked into Maurna's eyes welling with tears. He had made his decision.

No one knew how to close the Door, and someone was bound to open it even if it wasn't the Dragon's Voice. He claimed he would be a fair king, and maybe someone willing to do anything to bring peace to the world would be a good ruler. So Saim looked away from the mage, and walked to the altar.

"No," Maurna whimpered. "No! You can't do this!"

The half-elf paused to say, "I'd rather have you live in a world with Separ as king than have you die at his feet."

She continued to cry and beg Saim to reconsider, but he continued walking. He climbed the few steps behind the altar and fell to his knees on top of it. After positioning the tip of the blade over his chest, he took a moment to take one last look at the world he was leaving behind.

Maurna too was on her knees holding out her arms, and pleading for the half-elf to stop. Separ lowered Havish onto the bridge while he nodded sincerely at Saim. Behind the captain, the dragon continued to fight off the hoards of abysmyth climbing the walls. It was a world of pain, suffering, and war, and Saim knew he would miss it as he drove the sword into his chest.

All the sound began to muffle in the half-elf's scarred ears while he fell to his side. The mage ran to the altar screaming and placed her hands on his chest. The blackness began closing around his vision as Maurna cupped his jaw in her blood-soaked hands.

Behind her, Separ still stood over the bard with a solemn look on his face. Perhaps he didn't take joy in his own son's death.

"I will miss you," Saim whispered as he closed his eyes.

After only a moment, the eyes of the dragon carved into the large stone Door began to glow blue. From the sockets, cracks began to travel through the rock. Pieces of the door began to break off, but instead of falling to the ground, it seemed to be pulled into the glowing light behind it. Soon, all the fragments were sucked into the radiant blue illumination. The Door of Sight Unseen was open.

Maurna backed up while she glared into the swirling portal with fear. Separ stepped over Havish to finish his quest. Just as the captain pushed the mage aside and approached the altar, a burst of energy came from Saim's body, throwing Maurna and Separ to the ground, and woke Havish from his unconscious state.

As the pulse hit the walls of the volcano, the abysmyths crumbled apart, falling into the lava. It also forced the dragon to land at the opening of the room.

The bard shook his head to wake up, and instantly saw the dead half-elf atop the altar. Tears fell from his eyes, and he stumbled to his feet. He paid no mind to the lava far below as he ran to Saim's body, but just as he stepped off the stone bridge, the corpse started to float.

Finally, high above the altar, the half-elf became motionless in the air. The sword in his chest shot out and fell into the magma far below. Then a white light shined from the wound.

A bright orb slowly emerged from Saim's chest, and once it was free from the body, he fell back onto the altar. The white ball of light stayed in the air for only a moment, then flew into the portal, which closed immediately.

All was quiet as everyone stared at the wall where the portal had been. Separ got to his feet, still waiting for his reward. He walked to the wall impatiently, and a disappointed anger began to fill his shaking body.

"No," he growled, slamming his fists on the stone. "No! Where is it?"

"It's gone," sobbed Maurna. "*He's* gone."

"Where is my treasure?" cried Separ. "Damn you! I gave you my son!"

"You bastard!" hissed Havish with tears pouring down his cheeks. "You thought the voices of the Eye infallible, but even the abysmyths didn't know."

The pirate captain turned angrily to the bard. There was a hint of confusion on his face as he asked, "What are you talking about?"

Havish approached the altar and looked at the dead half-elf. He pushed Saim's hair away from his deformed ears, and placed his hand on the cheek of the corpse. The bard was overcome with a sadness he had only felt once before, and sobbed against the half-elf's chest. Maurna joined him in mourning over the body of the one they loved.

Separ's patience was wearing thinner, so he shouted, "Answer me!"

"He died never knowing the truth," mumbled Havish.

"Knowing what?" yelled the Dragon's Voice.

The bard looked up with a scowl, and with a lump in his throat, he told the captain, "He wasn't your son."

Chapter XXII

𝕬 sense of peace came over Saim. He knew he was dead, but it didn't bother him. When he opened his eyes, he could see he was no longer in the volcano. In fact, he wasn't even in the Southern Continent. The half-elf wasn't sure where he was, but it felt familiar.

Trees surrounded him, and a cool night breeze blew the leaves. It looked to be a forest in his home continent, but he wasn't sure where. He was able to see clearly in the moonlight as he glanced around. As he stood up from the tree he was sitting against, he noticed a yellow glow in the distance. Seeing the way shadows danced from the light, he could tell it was a small fire.

Saim pushed through low-hanging tree limbs toward the flame and eventually found himself at a campsite. The familiarity hit him even harder. There was a wagon with a horse attached and a man sleeping by the flame. A child stood over the unconscious person with his back toward the half-elf. Saim came closer, and saw bandages on the sides of the boy's head. The glow from the fire revealed the blood soaked into the cloth. This was when he noticed the dagger clutched in the boy's hands.

"Are you all right?" asked the half-elf.

Without turning away from the sleeping man, the child replied, "This was the moment. You knew the truth then, but you decided not to believe it."

"What?" said Saim.

It was at that point the half-elf saw the face of the sleeping man by the fire. He was much younger than the last time he had seen him. His hair and beard were still brown and had not yet been lightened by age. Havish.

Saim's face twisted in confusion, and he spun the child around to face him. He knew this child as well. He too was much younger, but then again, the half-elf couldn't remember the last time he had looked in a mirror. Still there was no denying he was looking at his younger self.

"What?" whispered Saim. "What is this?"

"You opened the Door," replied the child. "Now you get the reward."

"But Separ—"

"The pirate knew that to open the Door he would require a great sacrifice. But he put too much faith in the voices of the Eye. The abysmyths wanted only to protect the Door of Sight Unseen. They knew the only way to close it was in you."

"Why me?"

"Because you would provide the great sacrifice. Had you fought for your life, Separ would have killed you, and would reap the benefits of the Door. But for the lives of your friends, you took your own life."

Tears welled in Saim's eyes, but it was not sadness. It was the joy of knowing he had managed to end the chaos and save the ones he loved.

"Are you ready for your reward?" asked the child.

"What reward?"

"The truth."

"The truth about what?"

"All truths. Like me, you too will be all-knowing."

"Who are you?"

The child smirked, and replied with, "You already know who I am."

"The Great Spirit."

"That is your first truth," the boy said with a smile still on his face, "and there is the next."

The child pointed behind Saim, and the half-elf turned to see what he was motioning to. He found himself at a dock outside of a kingdom he had never seen before. Saim looked back to his younger self to ask where he was, but the child was no longer there. The half-elf searched the crowd of people walking around at all the shops along the pier, but his eyes rested on a large ship nearby. It was Separ's vessel, but it looked like it had barely touched the seas.

That's when Saim noticed a woman walking down the ramp leading off the boat and onto the dock. She had a hood over her head, so he wasn't sure who she was. All he could see was the blond hair hanging out from under it, but yet she kept his attention. He watched as she glanced around nervously just before making her way through the crowd.

Saim couldn't help but follow the mysterious woman as she browsed all the merchants. Eventually she entered the kingdom. She still looked over her shoulder as if she knew she was being followed and continued to a nearby inn.

Once inside, she walked up to the tavern bar and ordered a goblet of red wine. As she sat at a table to enjoy her drink, a flute began to play a joyful song. Saim turned to the source of the melody only to see an even-younger-looking Havish playing his instrument.

The intoxicated patrons of the tavern clapped along with the song, but one drunk seemed to be too busy eying the mysterious hooded woman to participate in the merriment. The inebriated man finally worked up the courage to stand, and walk over to the female's table. He attempted to introduce himself, but the woman showed no interest. This offended the man, so he sat across from her and tried to make conversation, but still she kept her head down.

Finally, the man had enough of being ignored, and he stood, throwing his chair to the ground. The room became quiet as he grabbed the woman's arm and pulled her close to him. Only seconds after she gasped in fear, the bard grabbed the drunk's shoulders and threw him onto an empty table which instantly collapsed.

"Are you all right?" Havish asked.

"Yes," replied the woman in a familiar voice.

The bard glared at the drunk fighting to stay conscious and said, "He won't stay down much longer. I think we'd best leave, lest you draw more unwanted attention to yourself."

Havish extended his hand to her, and after some thought, she grasped his hand and followed him from the tavern. Saim hurried behind them, but as soon as they ran out the front doors, the half-elf found himself in a different location completely.

The bard and woman were sitting at a table next to a lit fireplace in a small room with a bed. It looked to be a small home. Perhaps the Havish's.

When she finally removed the hood from her head, the bard could see why she wanted to be left alone. From beneath her blond hair, poked out two pointed ears. Saim moved around her to see her face. It was his mother. She and Havish spoke to one another, but Saim didn't listen.

"She had only known two humans to not judge her for her race," said a young voice behind the half-elf. "The other, of course, being Separ."

Saim spun to face his child-self, but he only ended up in another place. Creaking wood, the sound of water splashing outside, and the desk across the room from the bed led him to believe he was in a captain's quarters of a ship. Once he realized this was somewhere he had been before, Separ burst into the room with a dagger in hand.

He was younger, and didn't yet have the need for an eye patch. Fresh blood dripped off his blade and ran down his arms. He sat at his desk, and after planting the tip of his dagger into the thick wood in front of him, he pulled the Eye of Sight Unseen out of a leather pouch on his belt.

Lurya walked into the room, staring at the captain with fear as she made her way to the bed. The room was silent as she took a seat on the edge, still not taking her eyes off Separ. All that was heard was his heavy breathing as he stared at the red orb in his hand.

"You didn't have to kill him," whispered the elf.

"He was taking the Eye," mumbled the captain. "He was a thief and a traitor."

"You could have just taken him off the ship," she replied. "You control the dragons. There was no way he could have retaliated. We would have been safe."

"I couldn't show weakness to my crew, Lurya!" Separ yelled as he picked up the Eye and walked over to her. "If I let one man go without consequences, another could be inspired to take the Eye! One day, someone could be successful! Would you have them take our destiny from us?"

The captain stopped inches from her face, and she said in a shaking voice, "We wanted to end the violence. Not cause more."

"Peace has a price," he whispered, caressing her cheek with his bloody hand. "Don't you see that?"

She jerked her face away from him, and stared at the bed so not to meet his gaze. He scowled, stomped back to his desk, and pulled his dagger from the wood.

"You are a fool if you thought we could do this without violence!" he shouted, pointing at her with the still-wet blade. "I will do anything to ensure our victory! I will spill as much blood as it takes! Even my own!"

With that, Separ turned the dagger on himself, slicing deep into his face around his left eye. Both he and Lurya shrieked, one from agony, and the other from fright. Soon after, a puddle of crimson formed on the wooden floorboards, and he pulled his eye from his socket, cutting the attached nerve. As the captain panted from painful exhaustion, he took the Eye of Sight Unseen, and forced it into the open socket.

"What have you become?" the elf whimpered.

"I am the Dragon's Voice," grumbled the captain, "and I will rule this world."

Saim watched the tears glistening in his mother's eyes.

"This was the moment Lurya realized she was no longer in love," his younger self said.

The half-elf turned to the child and asked, "Why didn't she leave?"

"She did," explained the boy.

Behind the young half-elf, Saim could see he was back at the port. The large pirate vessel rested by a dock. Again he saw his mother in a hood sneaking off the boat. And again she went back into the kingdom. But this time she didn't go to the inn. She went to a small house nearby.

She knocked on the door, and after a few moments, someone opened it. It was Havish. He smiled and invited her inside. Once the bard shut the door, she took off her hood to reveal a bruise over her eye. Horrified, the human demanded to know what happened.

As she explained every detail, her eyes poured with sadness. The man that saved her life, and that she loved with all her heart, had become a monster. The bard comforted her with an innocent embrace and whispered in her ear that they could run. She protested and tried to explain what kind of danger this act would put him in. Still, he demanded they leave. Finally she agreed.

Saim watched them sneak out of the kingdom, then he saw the weeks they spent on the run from the searching eyes of Separ's men. They went from settlement to settlement, town to town, colony to colony, and kingdom to kingdom. Somewhere along their flight, they fell in love.

It wasn't much longer until she came to the realization that she had not had not bled since she and the bard had first made love. She knew she could not hide any longer, and decided the only way for the child to survive was to go back to Separ. Under the cover of night, she left the inn where she and the bard had rented a room. By the time he awoke, she was gone and back in the company of pirates.

The captain interrogated her for days, but once she said she was with child, his anger calmed. When she told him it was his, the anger disappeared, though his paranoia was stronger than ever. So he demanded that she never leave the boat again.

"Havish," whispered Saim. "He's my father."

"That is correct," replied the child, "but he didn't know, until the day Lurya returned to the bard's home."

When the half-elf tuned to his younger self, he saw blood dripping from the boy's back. Separ stood over the child with the leather straps in his hand. Saim remembered the beatings he had gotten when the captain thought he had the key needed to open the Door of Sight Unseen. The sight sent shivers through the half-elf's spine.

The child looked up, and went on to explain, "When your mother saw the danger you were in, she knew she had to get you off the ship."

Saim found himself in the bard's home once more, and he watched her tell the bard that he not only had a son, but that he had to hide his offspring from Separ. She made the plan to meet him in the woods on a morning not too far away, and explained that she could not go with him. He tried to find another way, but she knew she had to throw the captain off the trail.

When she returned to the ship, Separ found her sneaking on board. After throwing her back in her chambers where her son had woken up shortly before, she fed him a story of wanting some wine. It was enough to stop his violent interrogation, and he let her and the child be.

"Shortly after," the boy began, "you were delivered to Havish."

The child turned to look at the moment the bard and Lurya had to say goodbye for the last time. She let him know she would travel in the opposite direction, and Havish must not try to come back for her. She was going to her death. She knew it. He knew it. In some way their son knew it too.

After Havish left with the small half-elf, and they were farther away than she could see, Lurya collapsed and wept. When she finally collected herself, she began walking. She traveled all day and well into the night before Separ's men found her with their dragons.

There were weeks of agonizing interrogation, until she finally made up a story about how the bard was taking him to the Western Continent. Separ immediately set sail and scoured the land for Havish and young Saim. But he never found them.

Each passing day, the captain's anger grew, and the Eye brought him further and further from sanity. Realizing Lurya would never tell him the truth, he put her in chains and threw her overboard.

Tears poured from the adult half-elf's eyes as he watched her fight to stay above the water, and as her eyes closed, the child said, "And that's what brings us to this point."

As Saim turned he found himself again at the campsite with sleeping Havish. The boy's ears were bandaged again, and the dagger was back in his hand.

"You knew," the child uttered. "In some small way you knew he was your father, and that's why you didn't kill him."

Finally, Saim understood. The bard knew the bigotry of both man and elf, and he knew that a mixed race boy would only be easier for Separ to find. Havish only wanted to keep his son safe the only way he knew how. He removed the tips of his ears. The pain of having to hurt the child and lose his only love drove him to drown the agony with drink. He was never a bad father, he was just doing what he could to save the only thing he had left in this world. Something he loved so much, he thought it would be better off without him. So he stayed away, watching his son grow up without him.

"This is your second truth," said the boy. "Are you ready for more?"

"What else is there?" asked Saim, wiping tears from his eyes.

The child smiled, and whispered, "Everything."

Chapter XXIII

"**W**hat do you mean, he's not my son?" shouted Separ as he slowly walked away from the stone wall where the portal once was. "How could you know that?"

"Because I'm his father," Havish answered.

"Is that what Lurya told you?" laughed the captain. "As if you could trust a single syllable from that common strumpet."

"Say another cross word about her and it will be your last," growled the bard through his gritted teeth. "She was a mother willing to do whatever it took to save her son's life. Anything to keep him from you."

Havish placed his hand on Maurna's shoulder to comfort and mourn by the altar where Saim's body still lay. Separ approached the corpse and glared at it in disgust. The half-elf looked nothing like him, and he could no longer deny it.

"It's true. Isn't it?" mumbled the captain. "He may not be my boy, but I loved him as my own. With all my heart. Same as his mother."

"Is that why you killed them?" whimpered Maurna.

"For the first time in a while, the voices are quiet," Separ explained. "The Eye is silent, and only anger remains."

The bard met eyes with the captain and said, "I know the feeling."

Separ reached for Havish, but he backed away. Immediately, the captain snarled, and placed a foot atop the altar, launching himself at the bard. As Separ landed on Havish, he dealt blow after blow with his fists. Maurna tried to pull the Dragon's Voice off the bard, but he was much too powerful.

The captain turned, grabbed the mage by her collar, and pushed her hard into the side of the altar. Her head smacked the stone with such force, blood trailed off her temple and was lost into her raven hair.

She attempted to stand, but the room was spinning at such an alarming rate, she could only fall back against the altar. A high-pitched ringing was all that could be heard over the muffled sounds of the fighting humans.

Havish managed to get his leg under the captain and threw him back-first onto the bridge. The bard sprung back onto his feet and prepared to attack. Separ quickly stood to face his opponent, but the sound of his dragon screeching behind him caught his attention.

Everyone turned to see the winged monster fall to the ground with fresh blood spewing from its neck, which now had a large ax in it. Next to the slayed beast stood Rust spotted with the dark red liquid. Some was his. Some was Porter's. The rest tasted of sweet revenge.

The dwarf looked to Separ and pulled his weapon free of the scales. He started his slow, limping approach across the stone bridge. His breathing was heavy from the agony of every step, but the fire burning in his heavy heart kept him going.

"So you killed one dragon," the captain announced. "It matters not. I have more on the way. Soon this place will be crawling with them."

"You killed my oldest friend," groaned Rust. "I don't suppose you know how that feels, since you've killed everyone in your life who was idiotic enough to care for you. But you will know my pain. You will know it tenfold."

The dwarf picked up the pace and raised his ax over his head. Then, with all the strength he had left in his broken body, he brought his weapon down. But the blade stopped in front of Separ's face as the captain grabbed the handle. Then the Dragon's Voice put his boot into Rust's chest and pushed him to the ground keeping the dwarf's ax in his grasp.

Havish rushed onto the bridge to assist the dwarf, but the captain spun to swing his newly obtained weapon. The bard jumped back, barely evading the sharp edge. Then Havish cocked his fist for an attack, but Separ struck him across the nose with the handle of the ax.

The bard stumbled backward and finally fell on his side next to the edge of the bridge. Havish's eyes widened as he looked at the boiling molten rock far below and quickly pushed himself onto his back. He saw the captain standing over him with the ax ready to cleave his abdomen. Havish could only shut his eyes, because he knew it was too late to get out of the way.

Maurna still struggled to stay conscious, but the sight of the bard in peril forced her to recover. Her legs were shaking, and she couldn't get traction under her feet. She felt too weak to stand. Helpless. But after a few more attempts at getting up, the gentle touch of a hand on her shoulder stopped her.

Before Havish could be hit with the blade of Separ's weapon, the captain suddenly groaned in pain. He began to pant as the torment subsided, and he once again prepared to finish the bard off. But another wave of pain shot through the captain's skull.

Separ dropped the ax and covered the orb in his socket with his hands. He stumbled and screamed with such volume it shook the whole mountain. When the captain finally collapsed to his knees, he caught a glimpse of the cause of his pain. It was something he couldn't believe he was seeing. But there it was. The half-elf sat up with his hand on the mage's shoulder.

Saim turned to Separ and hopped off the altar. Slowly, the half-elf walked onto the bridge. Blood still ran from the sword wound in his chest, but he strolled on as if he felt nothing. He just stared into the captain's eye as he came closer.

The pain became so intense that it forced every vein in Separ's body against his skin, and he dropped his arms to his side. Then after a spray of blood, the Eye of Sight Unseen came out of his socket. It hovered in front of his face, dripping with blood. The captain glared at his reflection in the red jewel as it floated to Saim.

The orb entered the wound in the half-elf's chest, which began to close up. Saim stood still watching the horrified expression on Separ's red pained face. Soon after the bleeding hole healed, the half-elf felt his scarred ears tingle. His hair was pushed aside as the cartilage shaped back into the points he had not had since he was a child.

Maurna and Havish stared at him in awe and confusion. It was Saim, but the look in his eyes was different. It was a look of someone wiser. Someone brave. Someone stronger. Someone who could not lose.

"How?" asked the captain in a shaking voice.

"I have lived several lifetimes in the Abyss," said the half-elf calmly. "But I had to leave. I had to come back. I had to stop you."

Separ was angry, but his curiosity made him grunt out the question, "What? What was it like? What is the treasure of the Door of Sight Unseen."

"Truth," replied Saim. "The knowledge of everything that has ever been, or ever will."

"Truth?" shouted the former Dragon's Voice. "That's it? That's the treasure?"

"Yes," answered the half-elf as he took a few more steps toward Separ. "And here is your truth."

Saim placed his hand on the captain's head and showed him the pain he had caused in his lifetime. Separ screamed as he felt the suffering of every man, woman, and child of every race that had been affected by his tyranny. Sons, daughters, and widows devastated over the loss of their fathers and husbands. The anguish of his enemies as blades tore their flesh. A mother terrified of the danger her son faced aboard his ship. A half-elf's agony as he was beaten for information about the Door of Sight Unseen.

"Enough!" cried the captain as he pushed away Saim's hand.

"Truth..." whispered the half-elf. "It is the most powerful weapon one can have. That is the Treasure of Sight Unseen."

Tears ran from Separ's eye and down his blood-covered cheek. Even cutting out his own eye didn't compare to the torture he had just endured. He knew that people were hurt in his path, but the magnitude of all that at one time was too much to bear. How could he have thought he would make a great leader with the things he had done? It was too heavy. Too much to go on from here.

"Kill me," Separ ordered. "I've earned. It's all I have earned."

Havish, Rust, and Maurna couldn't comprehend it. The captain was defeated. Not just foiled, but broken in spirit. To spill Separ's blood now would have meant nothing. He was harmless. Destroyed.

Then the dwarf had one thought, one name that echoed in his mind. Porter. How he raised the boar since he was almost new to this world, the nights they would sleep against one another, the warmth of his face when he would rub his snout across the dwarf's cheek, and the tired look in Porter's eyes before he closed them just a short while ago. One recollection of those memories was all the motivation Rust needed to stand, pick up his ax, and take off Separ's head.

As the body collapsed, as if a puppeteer had released his strings, his severed skull fell far below into the lava. The dwarf took but a moment to let the sweetness of it all soak in before kicking the decapitated corpse off the bridge to be devoured by the molten rock as well. The Door of Sight Unseen was shut. The Dragon's Voice was gone.

Saim helped the man he now knew to be his father onto his feet, and looked into his eyes. Havish was speechless. He could only quiver his lip as tears of rejoice made their way into his beard.

"My mother..." the half-elf began. "She was so grateful for your help. And even more for your love."

"You know?" the bard asked.

"Yes," replied Saim. "And I also know why you didn't tell me."

"I'm sorry," whispered Havish.

"Don't be," responded the half-elf. "You were right. Had you said you were my father, I would have given my life for you at the first sign of danger."

His father smiled and said, "But you did it without knowing."

"Not only for you," said Saim as he turned to look at Maurna. "It was for her too."

The mage smiled as the half-elf came to her and lifted her from the ground. She remained still for a while, looking deep into his irises. That's when she saw through the slight change his manner had made, and noticed his pureness underneath. He was still the humble Saim she had come to care about despite what he had been through. He was alive. And he was hers.

She embraced him so tightly, it almost knocked the half-elf off his feet. Once he had steadied himself, he too returned the affection. Through his shirt he felt her warm tears on his chest. Her sobs proving to her how strongly she felt for this half-elf. A love so pure for an abomination.

Saim leaned closer, and in his love's ear he whispered, "Let's go."

With that, he turned and led his father, Rust, and Maurna out of the room. For the first time, they felt like they weren't racing to a purpose, or running from danger.

Once they reached the entrance in the mountain, they stopped to allow Rust to mourn the loss of his boar. Saim understood the sadness in the dwarf's heart, because the half-elf seen the bond they had shared while he was in the Abyss. Rust refused any medical attention to his many injuries until he buried his oldest friend. Despite the dwarf's protest, Maurna, Saim, and Havish helped him find stones to cover the shell where Porter once dwelled.

It took a while to finish the grave, but once complete, Rust lay his hand upon the stones, and said under his breath, "I'm sorry."

After the dwarf took a little more time saying goodbye to his loyal ally, the ground began to shake as if many heavy things were dropped outside the mountain. Rust, the mage, and the bard became uneasy, but the smile on the half-elf's face only confused them.

"What is that?" grumbled the dwarf.

"Our ride home," replied Saim as he walked out of the cave.

Havish, Maurna, and Rust followed the half-elf outside, and were taken off-guard by what was awaiting them. Three dragons stood tall by the entrance into the mountain, and all of their scaly, horned faces were looking directly at them.

Saim didn't appear afraid as he slowly raised his hand to the beast standing closest to him. Suddenly, the creature lowered its head, which caused everyone to gasp. As Rust's grip tightened on his ax, he realized the dragon was staying still so the half-elf could pet his nose.

The other two winged beasts bowed their heads low to the ground, and Saim turned to his fellow travelers to say, "I summoned them here. They are to take us home."

"Where is home?" Maurna asked.

"Wherever we want it to be."

Epilogue

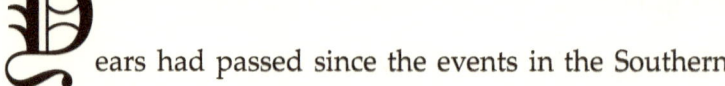ears had passed since the events in the Southern

Continent, but the story never lost interest among all people. It

was the tale of how the brave half-elf, his human father, an elven

mage, and a dwarven sellsword forgot all prejudice so they

could save the world from an evil pirate. Bards in all the king-

doms, settlements, and colonies in all four continents told their

audiences the story in their own way, adding more and more

embellishments as time passed, but no one told it with the

passion Havish could, because only he knew it was only the

truth.

Every time the half-elf's father told the tale, it would get

longer. This was not due to exaggerations that other bards would

include. It was updates on his son, the elf, and the dwarf.

The first addition to the story was how Rust returned to

his home. Though he was met only with disdain at first, his

fellow dwarves began to accept him when he brought prosperity

back to Runehelm. With the abysmyths no longer a threat, and

the dragons now free from having to drive the monsters

underground, the mines were reopened. The sellsword ended

his mercenary life, and spent the rest of his days rich beyond his wildest dreams. He was always charitable with his wealth, and he never forgot his boar, Porter. In fact, in the center of the settlement was a golden statue of the majestic beast. Regardless, the most important moment in Rust's life was the day his brother, Kragg, forgave him.

The next addition was about the few survivors of Naughstaure. They rebuilt their homes, and with the help of Maurna, Kymay, and her love, it grew back into the magnificent kingdom it once was. It was the first time since before the war that humans and dwarves could travel through Naughstaure for trade. It was also the first time in history they accepted a half-elf as their king ruling next to his mage queen.

The last addition to the bard's story was added shortly before his death. It was the day Havish met his grandchild on the day of her birth. Maurna and Saim decided on the name that pleased the half-elf's father immensely. Lurya.

On the night the bard passed, he was surrounded by his family. He was not afraid to die, because he had lived a life in which he followed his heart. He loved, and he was loved. It was the perfect way to leave the world. But before he went on to meet the Great Spirit, he told Saim he should not mourn, for he would never truly die.

Of course the half-elf grieved for a period, but he always understood what his father meant. The story would go on through the mouths and into the ears of the living. In that way, Havish was immortal, as were all the travelers. Even when they too passed, they would reunite in the Abyss many years later.

The world was at peace, and the ones that saved it were never forgotten.